To the Musers,
who know this was a group effort

Break

Break

Hannah Moskowitz

Simon Pulse

New York   London   Toronto   Sydney

SIMON PULSE

An imprint of Simon & Schuster Children's Publishing Division

1230 Avenue of the Americas, New York, NY 10020

First Simon Pulse paperback edition August 2009

Copyright © 2009 by Hannah Moskowitz

All rights reserved, including the right of reproduction in whole or in part in any form.

SIMON PULSE and colophon are registered trademarks of Simon & Schuster, Inc.

For information about special discounts for bulk purchases, please contact

Simon & Schuster Special Sales at 1-866-506-1949 or business@simonandschuster.com.

The Simon & Schuster Speakers Bureau can bring authors to your live event. For more information or to book an event contact the Simon & Schuster Speakers Bureau at 1-866-248-3049 or visit our website at www.simonspeakers.com.

Designed by Mike Rosamilia

The text of this book was set in Manticore.

Manufactured in the United States of America

10 9 8 7 6 5 4 3 2 1

Library of Congress Control Number 2008042816

ISBN 978-1-4169-8275-3

ISBN 978-1-4391-5906-4 (eBook)

Acknowledgments

The ever-fabulous Jenoyne Adams and Anica Rissi, Amanda K. Morgan, Chris, Alex, Emma, Galen, Seth, Abby, Mom and Dad, Motion City Soundtrack, Alexander Supertramp, and Chuck Palahniuk. Thanks for the inspiration.

one

THE FIRST FEELING IS EXHILARATION.

My arms hit the ground. The sound is like a mallet against a crab.

Pure fucking exhilaration.

Beside me, my skateboard is a stranded turtle on its back. The wheels shriek with each spin.

And then—oh. *Oh*, the pain.

The second feeling is pain.

Naomi's camera beeps and she makes a triumphant noise in her throat. "You *totally* got it that time," she says. "Tell me you got it."

I hold my breath for a moment until I can say, "We got it."

"You fell like a bag of mashed potatoes." Her sneakers make bubble gum smacks against the pavement on her way to me. "Just . . . splat."

So vivid, that girl.

Naomi's beside me, and her tiny hand is an ice cube on my smoldering back.

"Don't get up," she says.

I choke out a sweaty, clogged piece of laughter. "Wasn't going to, babe."

"Whoa, you're bleeding."

"Yeah, I thought so." Blood's the unfortunate side effect of a hard-core fall. I pick my head up and shake my neck, just to be sure I can. "This was a definitely a good one."

I let her roll me onto my back. My right hand stays pinned, tucked grotesquely under my arm, fingers facing back toward my elbow.

She nods. "Wrist's broken."

"Huh, you think?" I swallow. "Where's the blood?"

"Top of your forehead."

I sit up and lean against Naomi's popsicle stick of a body and wipe the blood off my forehead with my left hand. She gives me a quick squeeze around the shoulders, which is basically as affectionate as Naomi gets. She'd probably shake hands on her deathbed.

She takes off her baseball cap, brushes back her hair, and replaces the cap with the brim tilted down. "So what's the final tally, kid?"

Ow. Shit. "Hold on a second."

She waits while I pant, my head against my skinned knee. Colors explode in the back of my head. The pain's almost electric.

"Hurt a lot?" she asks.

I expand and burst in a thousand little balloons. "Remind me why I'm doing this again?"

"Shut up, you."

I manage to smile. "I know. Just kidding."

"So what hurts? Where's it coming from?"

"My brain."

She exhales, rolling her eyes. "And your brain is getting these pain signals from where, sensei?"

"Check my ankles." I raise my head and sit up, balancing on my good arm. I suck on a bloody finger and click off my helmet. The straps flap around my chin. I taste like copper and dirt.

I squint sideways into the green fluorescence of the 7-Eleven. No one inside has noticed us, but it's only a matter of time. Damn. "Hurry it up, Nom?"

She takes each of my sneakered feet by the toe and moves it carefully back and forth, side to side, up and down. I close my eyes and feel all the muscles, tendons, and bones shift perfectly.

"Anything?"

I shake my head. "They're fine."

"Just the wrist, then?"

"No. There's something else. It-it's too much pain to be just the wrist. . . . It's somewhere. . . ." I gesture weakly.

"You seriously can't tell?"

"Just give me a second."

Naomi never gets hurt. She doesn't understand. I think she's irritated until she does that nose-wrinkle. "Look, we're not talking spinal damage or something here, right? Because I'm going to feel really shitty about helping you in your little mission if you end up with spinal damage."

I kick her to demonstrate my un-paralysis.

She smiles. "Smart-ass."

I breathe in and my chest kicks. "Hey. I think it's the ribs."

Naomi pulls up my T-shirt and checks my chest. While she takes care of that, I wiggle all my fingers around, just to check. They're fine—untouched except for scrapes from the pavement. I dig a few rocks from underneath a nail.

"I'm guessing two broken ribs," she says.

"Two?"

"Yeah. Both on the right."

I nod, gulping against the third feeling—nausea.

"Jonah?"

I ignore her and struggle to distract myself. Add today to the total, and that's 2 femurs + 1 elbow + 1 collarbone + 1 foot + 4 fingers + 1 ankle + 2 toes + 1 kneecap + 1 fibula + 1 wrist + 2 ribs.

= 17 broken bones.

189 to go.

Naomi looks left to the 7-Eleven. "If we don't get out of here soon, someone's going to want to know if you're okay. And then we'll have to find another gross parking lot for next time."

"Relax. I'm not doing any more skateboard crashes."

"Oh, yeah?"

"Enough with the skateboard. We've got to be more creative next time, or your video's gonna get boring."

She makes that wicked smile. "You okay to stand?" She takes my good hand and pulls me up. My right wrist dangles off to the side like the limb of a broken marionette. I want to hold it up, but Naomi's got me in a death grip so I won't fall.

My stomach clenches. I gasp, and it kills. "Shit, Nom."

"You're okay."

"I'm gonna puke."

"Push through this. Come on. You're a big boy."

Any other time, I would tease her mercilessly for this comment. And she knows it. Damn this girl.

I'm upright, but that's about as far as I'm going to go. I lean against the grody wall of the Laundromat. "Just bring the car around. I can't walk that far."

She makes her hard-ass face. "There's nothing wrong with your legs. I'm not going to baby you."

My mouth tastes like cat litter. "Nom."

She shakes her hair and shoves down the brim of her cap. "You really do look like crap."

She always expects me to enjoy this part. She thinks a boy who likes breaking bones has to like the pain.

Yeah. Just like Indiana Jones loves those damn snakes.

I do begging eyes.

"All right," she says. "I'll get the car. Keep your ribs on."

This is Naomi's idea of funny.

She slouches off. I watch her blur into a lump of sweatshirt, baseball cap, and oversize jeans.

Shit. Feeling number four is worry. Problems carpet bomb my brain.

What am I going to tell my parents? How is this setting a good example for Jesse? What the hell am I doing in the grossest parking lot in the city on a Tuesday night?

The feeling that never comes is regret.

There's no room. Because you know you're three bones closer.

two

AT THE HOSPITAL, I CALL HOME. MOM ANSWERS
with, "Jesse has hives."

So weird. I could be anyone. She could be announcing
my brother's skin condition to a telemarketer.

I smile at the nurse as she takes my vitals. The blood
pressure machine beeps.

I think, *Of course he has hives.* Jesse has reactions to
almost everything. Will's baby food is everywhere. So
yeah. Jesse's going to get hives.

But I just say, "How's his breathing?"

"Oh, you listen. I never know."

I roll my eyes and wait for Jesse to get on the phone.
"Blood pressure's a little high," Nurse tells me.

Naomi flips a page in her magazine. "Breaking a few bones will do that to ya."

I kick her. "I feel fine," I tell Nurse. "Thanks."

Jesse picks up the phone and says, "Hey, brother."

We call each other "brother" like it's our name. Sometimes I worry we'll forget our real ones.

I actually worry about things like this.

I say, "How you feeling?" while the nurse looks at my ribs.

"I'm fine. Mom's overreacting."

I believe him, because Jess is good about admitting when he's not fine. He's basically good about most things. And he's breathing in and out, nice and slow.

"Yeah, you're fine." Some machine nearby starts beeping and I hold the phone tighter against my cheek to block the receiver.

Still, Jesse says, "Do I hear hospital noises?"

It's sad that he can recognize them so well. Not to mention inconvenient. I don't answer.

He groans. "Man, come on."

"I was just about to tell you. Honestly."

"Uh-huh." He exhales, all smooth and clean. "So what'd you get?"

"Broken wrist, a couple broken ribs."

The nurse tells Naomi the doctor will be here soon and swooshes out through the curtain.

Jess says, "Shit, Jonah."

"No, hush. It's not that bad. How're Mom and Dad?"

"They yelled about the baby for a while and now they're having a truce. Which I'm sure will be temporary when they find out you've broken yourself. Again."

"I'll tell them I fell off my skateboard," I mumble, lying back on the bed.

"And really you . . ."

"Fell off my skateboard, actually."

"This has got to stop."

"Yeah. It'll stop. I promise." One hundred and eighty-nine bones from now. The baby wail builds like a siren.

I squeeze my eyes shut as my wrist grinds. Will was born eight months ago, and he has cried ever since.

I understand that most babies cry. But I've decided the reason you're supposed to have kids close together in age is so they don't care when their little siblings wail. When I was a year old, what the hell did I care if baby Jess was screaming?

But now I'm seventeen and Jess is sixteen and when our little brother cries, we worry.

When he cries for eight months, we worry for eight months.

Will hiccups and wails right into the phone. Jess is holding him, even though he's not supposed to.

"You shouldn't hold him if he's been breastfeeding," I say.

Naomi clears her throat. "The baby? Again?"

Naomi is very disdainful of Will, probably in the same way she's jealous of Jesse. When you come from a non-family, it's very easy to resent someone whose brothers take up his whole life. I get it, but that doesn't mean I tolerate it, and I wave her away.

"He could still spit up on you," I say. "Come on. You've got hives."

Jesse says, "I can't believe we're discussing this now. You're in the fucking hospital, Jonah."

And Mom says, "He's *where?*"

I wince. "Smooth."

"Shit," he mumbles.

"Nice going."

"I wasn't thinking."

And now Mom's screaming and the baby's screaming and Jess is yelling back and I just say, "I'll call you later," and hang up.

Thirty seconds later, my phone starts vibrating, extra hard like it can gauge the urgency of the call. A white coat brushes in through the door and raises his eyebrows.

"You're not supposed to have cell phones in here," he says.

I shut it off gratefully.

three

MY PARENTS HAVE HOME-FROM-THE-ER FACES.
Dad starts his as soon as we walk through the front door,
and Mom mirrors even though she stayed home and
bounced the baby. They wear them all through dinner,
scraping their water-spotted silverware against the plates.
Jesse is gathering the ingredients for a shake. One of his
usual meals. None of them talks. I sit on the bar. They're
my play of a family, and I'm their attentive audience. Just
like always.

Will bangs his fists on the high chair and cries into
his sweet potatoes. Mom forces the baby spoon between
his lips and he spits all over her.

Turns out my jaw is broken too, and now it's wired

shut. My tongue is a dead fish in the center of my mouth, but I talk anyway. "It was just an accident," I say, as best I can. "I'm an idiot. I'll try to be more careful."

"We worry about you," Dad says, in that thin-as-onionskin voice.

"He's fine," Jesse says. "Look at him."

They look at me. I make my biggest smile, and the wires pull between my teeth.

Mom chews. "He's getting a black eye."

"So I'll look like a prizefighter for a few days. There are worse fates, Mom. Will, shhh." I wipe orange mush out of his black black baby hair and immediately lean over to the sink to wash my hands. I glance at Jess.

He empties two packets of brown powder into the blender, one for each of us. I don't ask what it is. Jess makes proteins shakes all the time—and swears he likes them—but it's still nice of him to share his dinner with me just because I can't chew. Especially when he, unlike Mom and Dad, knows I did this to myself.

He starts the blender and watches the sludge stir around.

The deal with Jesse is that he has food allergies. I don't mean like those kids who get a little blotchy when they eat peanuts. And I really don't mean like those moms who say little Timmy can't handle Red 40.

Jess's throat closes up if he eats eggs. Or wheat. Or milk. Or fish. Or nuts, chocolate, strawberries.

Or basically anything.

His blood pressure drops and he swells right up and he can go from fine to dead in less than three minutes. He doesn't even need to eat the stuff. Touching or breathing it is enough.

I can't remember everything he's allergic to. The list is too fucking long. Really, I just freak out if I see him eating. Sometimes I'll freak out when he's drinking bottled water. It's just a reflex.

Will babbles among his screams and shakes his head when Mom pushes more potatoes.

"He's always a little banged up now." Dad cuts a bite of lamb and stuffs it into his mouth. "People are going to talk."

I stretch my arm out, examining the cast. "If they ask, I'll just tell them Jesse did it."

Mom snorts. "You'd be in even more pieces if Jesse did it."

Jesse's captain of the hockey team, first string for soccer, starting center in basketball. He's four inches taller than I am and fifty pounds heavier—all muscle— and not quite as good-looking, but let's face it. He's not lacking.

The boy's sort of a god. He's got a miniature freshman cult following. And yeah, he could rip me to shreds if he wanted to.

Jesse laughs. "She's right. You'd have a lot worse than a cast and a band around your ribs, boy."

"Don't forget the jaw."

"How can you even understand what he's saying?" Mom complains, spearing a bite of meat at the end of her fork. "He sounds like he's talking with his mouth full."

Dad shovels in more lamb as potatoes splurt out the sides of his lips.

Mom puts her hands over her eyes. "This is all over the parenting books. You've got one child with special needs, the other one has to act out."

I wonder where that leaves the baby.

Jess makes noises in his throat. "Don't call me special needs, God. I sound like I should be drooling in a wheelchair."

"Lord's name in vain, Jesse!"

He rolls his eyes.

I say, "I am not competing with Jesse."

Jesse revs the blender one last time. Will raises his voice to compensate.

Jesse pours our smoothie into two glasses and hands one to me. I get a straw so I can wedge it between my teeth, and Jesse chugs his. His Adam's apple bobs. He makes drinking look like an Olympic sport.

I gag, which feels sort of dangerous and exhilarating with the broken jaw. "This tastes like crap."

"You get used to it." Jesse plunks his empty glass down on the counter and heads toward his room. He strolls past Mom and Dad's steaming plates of poison, his chin in the air.

Will says, "Bababa," in that teary voice, and Mom and Dad start arguing again.

So I enjoy my smoothie.

four

IT STARTED LAST YEAR WITH THE CAR ACCIDENT.

Mom was driving, I was shotgun, Jesse was in the back. On the way to a doctor's appointment.

Mom ran a red light—barely—and we slammed into an overanxious cement truck. Mom was six or seven months pregnant at the time.

To this day, the smell of wet pavement makes me sick.

Mom got a nasty burn on her leg from the airbag, but no problems with the baby. Jesse was, for once, basically fine. I was the one who went sideways and broke through the latch on the door of Mom's shitty van.

Jesse's lip bled where he bit it through, and he looked

like something from a horror movie when he knelt over me. He said, "Don't move." He said it over and over and over, like I'd try to sit up the second he was quiet.

Like I *could* sit up.

I broke 2 femurs + 1 elbow + 1 collarbone.

I don't know what bones hit against the door, what I smashed falling into the street. I don't know why it was me and not Mom and Jesse and Will the Fetus. I'd never broken anything before.

But I'd been in a shitload of ambulances before with Jesse, so that, at least, was normal. If not comforting.

All of a sudden my life was emergency room, splints, surgery, physical therapy. It was like a fucking Discovery Health special.

At the hospital, everyone thinks about dying. And I'd never been much for romanticizing death—especially not suicide. I'd always been a fan of staying alive.

After all, you basically do all you can to not die. All the time. The search for immortality isn't just from storybooks. Every day you do it. You buckle your seatbelt, you take vitamin supplements, look both ways before you cross the street. And you really think you're doing all you can. Bullshit. We can lift weights for fucking hours and we're still going to die.

And I didn't truly get that until I was in the middle

of a highway with a tailpipe between my legs, slathered in cement.

At the hospital, the answer's all around you. You have to fight for your life. It's the only way.

You only get so many chances to be destroyed. Got to make the most of them.

You've probably read that broken bones grow back stronger. It's sort of a natural bionics thing. Break a leg, grow a better leg. Break a body, grow a better body.

The worse you're hurt, the stronger you get. I see that every day in Jesse Who Will Not Die.

So I was lying in the street, I was broken, and I was fixed.

I was barely through with the mess from the car accident when I crashed my mountain bike during some trick. I'd always been a daredevil. No one was surprised I'd had a spill.

And it was just a spill. Just a mistake.

Of course.

It was a mistake worth 1 foot + 4 fingers + 1 ankle + 2 toes.

Naomi was there for that one. She drove me to the hospital and was catatonic the whole way.

"It was fucking beautiful," she finally squeaked while the ER people pulled on my limbs. "The way you just flew . . . it was like art. I wish I'd had my damn camera."

"Well," I said. "Maybe next time."

So the next time, she helped me set up the skate ramp. And I let her film. And we started trying to fall. And four falls later, we got it—1 kneecap + 1 fibula.

"Holy shit," Naomi said. "You just broke your leg."

"Anything for art, babe."

It's been about six months since I haven't had something in a cast. Kids at school laugh and call me a klutz. This girl Charlotte carries my books. My parents are baffled. Will cries. Jesse keeps getting sick.

You're broken, and you're fixed.

And you're better.

five

I'M FILLING OUT THE SPREADSHEET WHEN NAOMI CALLS.

"You know each foot has twenty-six bones," she says. "So just 'broken foot' doesn't really count."

"It's good enough for me." I type in 1 broken jaw. Total = 18. I'm seriously going to need to practice this one-handed typing. It's almost as annoying as the whole talking-with-my-mouth-closed thing. "Do you have any idea how many bones there are in your fingers? If I tried for every single tiny bone, I'd be insane."

"Yeah, *then* you'd be insane. You know your voice is ridiculous. You sound drunk."

"Wish I felt drunk."

"So how'd the parents handle it?"

"Oh, the usual. They hate hospitals, obviously."

"Obviously."

"They've got to realize this isn't about them. I wish there was some way to keep them out of it entirely. Or to explain it to them without scaring them shitless."

"You can't explain this, Jonah."

"I know I can't."

She's quiet. Naomi walks this fine line between enabling me and cautioning me. Between daring me and mothering me. When she gets too close to either extreme, she's got to shut up. It's the only way.

"I'm fine," I tell her.

She does this irritating sigh thing. "I didn't ask. So my video's fucking awesome."

"Yeah?" I pull my shirt up and look at the huge piece of elastic around my ribs. It feels like I'm wearing a corset, which isn't as unpleasant as you might think. I wonder if I have to sleep in this thing. I wonder if it hurts if I poke it.

Yep.

She says, "Yeah. You look like fucking Silly Putty hitting the sidewalk. And you can totally hear your wrist shatter."

"It's not shattered. Just fractured. Shatter would mean surgery." There's a knock on my door. "Hold on. Jess?"

He pokes his head in and waves. There's a baby on his shoulder.

"Yeah, it's just Jess. Come in."

He sits on my bed and bounces, looking through the books on my nightstand. "More Confucianism?" he says.

I cover the speaker. "It's interesting. Give him to me."

Jess shakes his head and gives Will a squeeze. "I think he's quieting down now."

"You cannot keep touching him. He is giving you hives. Look at you."

Jess stretches his arms out and examines his skin. "I'm fine."

"Hold on a minute, Nom." I set down the phone and hold my hands out for the baby. Jess relinquishes him. "Go wash your hands," I order, rocking whiny Will back and forth. "Take more Benadryl."

He doesn't stand up, just murmurs to himself as he flips through the pages of my book. "I'm going to turn into Benadryl."

I return to Naomi. "Sorry."

"How's Jesse?"

I say, "Jesse, how are you?"

He shrugs.

"He's all right."

"Tell her hi," he mumbles, turning a page.

Naomi says, "Jesus Christ. Isn't Will a little old to cry this much?"

"Well. Yeah."

Jesse shifts awkwardly, showing no signs of leaving.

Naomi's back to the subject at hand. "You just slam against the pavement. That's the exciting part. The collision. The whole fall is anticipation, then—wham."

"Do you have my groan of pain?"

"I have no groan, no. I have you whining like a little girl."

"Edit that out." I raise my eyebrows to Jesse and mouth, *Need something?*

"Uh-uh." He's got this little mustache growing in. It looks like he hasn't washed his face. I mime shaving and he shakes his head vigorously.

"You're not even listening," Naomi complains.

"Oh, be quiet."

She hangs up. I smile and lower the phone into its cradle. "What's up, kid?"

Jesse stretches out with his feet on my pillow. "Checking up on you. How's the wrist?"

"Fine."

"And the ribs?"

"Fine."

"And the jaw?"

"Well, you know."

Will slips against my cast. It's hard to hold a baby with one arm and a chest that feels like it's collapsing.

Jesse shakes his head. "You're an idiot. Mom and Dad are freaking out about you."

"You should be happy they're not bugging you so much."

"Yeah, I would be. If my big brother didn't have to be a broken fucking idiot to make them leave me alone."

Jesse won't give up the idea that I'm doing this for him.

I really can be selfish, Jess.

"Just be careful, okay?" he says.

"Okay."

He leaves, and I set Will on my lap so I can jot down which bones I'm going to break next. + 1 hand + 8 toes + 1 cheekbone. Total = 28.

six

I COULD BREAK MY FUCKING NECK AND MY MORNING routine wouldn't change. Alarm at 5:57. Lay in bed until six listening to the squeaky-squeak of Jess on the rowing machine and the roar of baby Will that's kept me awake since two in the morning. Sit up and feel dizzy.

No. Wait. The dizziness is new.

Ugh.

Will's even louder when my head's off the pillow.

My mouth feels like I've been chewing on broken glass. The wrist is fine, but my chest is vibrating, it's throbbing so hard. *God*, I need a day off.

But pussying out is so not the point.

I trudge downstairs and start boiling some water. Mom's at the table, trying to get Will to drink.

"Maybe it's an ear infection!" I shout over his screams.

She shakes her head. "Doctor said his ears look fine."

"Did they check his throat? Maybe it's a cold."

"No fever."

What kind of cold lasts eight months, anyway?

I gesture to the milk dribbling down Will's chin. "You've got to clean him up. Jesse will be coming up for breakfast."

Jesse's so allergic to milk that Mom can barely touch him now that she's breastfeeding. She showers before she hugs him. But still, she'll leave Will's bottles and baby food lying around, like she forgets she has more than one son.

She sighs. "God, this place is a mess."

"Yeah, it is. Look, you've got to be more careful, Mom." Jesse starts coughing downstairs and I say, "Listen."

"I know."

"It's awful for him. He was actually pretty healthy before you had Will." And since then we've been in fucking allergy hell.

"I know, Jonah."

I take out a sponge and start wiping down the

counters. "Can't you start weaning the baby? Put him on rice milk?"

"Rice milk's not good for babies."

"It'll give him what, a toothache?" I hold up the soaked sponge. "Doesn't exactly compare to one of Jess's reactions, does it?"

"I know, I know." She stands up, Will in the crook of her arm. "I'll take him upstairs."

"Thank you."

Once she's gone, and Will's screams fade into her bedroom, I take Benadryl and steroids and inhalers and shit out of the cupboard and line them up by Jesse's placemat. It's not easy to open the pill bottles with one hand, but I get over it. I take two Cokes from the fridge and tromp down to the basement, palming them both in my one good hand.

Jesse is drenched and glued to the rowing machine. I toss his Coke to him and he catches it in his left hand. Coke's about the only thing we can share.

"You're a force, brother," I say.

"Don't I know it." He scratches his neck, but stops before I can yell at him. He says, "You're, uh, kind of slurring your words, there."

"I know, I know."

Jesse follows me upstairs, throws the pills down his

throat and chases them with a mouthful of Coke. I pour a glass of orange juice for myself and fill a cup from the tap for Jesse. I really feel like an omelet, but you can't fry eggs when Jesse is home. Airborne proteins and all that. Crazy stuff.

The whole kitchen smells like his sweat. Sixteen-year-old guys smell like deodorant and fast food. Then you turn seventeen and you get fresh.

"You making oatmeal?" he asks.

"Yep. I'm going to drink it through a *straw*."

"Bad. Ass."

"Don't I know it, brother."

I figure if I've got to eat stuff Jesse's allergic to right in front of him—and if I didn't, I'd never eat—I should make it something gross whenever possible. It's hard to be jealous of oatmeal.

The water boils and I dump a packet of instant oatmeal in a bowl. Jesse watches me shave bananas and cinnamon while he makes his smoothie. Fake milk. Protein powder. Vitamins he needs to get and can't otherwise. Applesauce. He blends and the concoction turns brown. Just like every day.

I suck out the thinner bits of the oatmeal through the straw. Jesse drinks and watches me, snickering.

"Shut up." I wipe my lips. "Do you have practice today?"

He nods. "Hockey's, like, our whole life right now. We're totally falling behind in school and shit."

Jesse always speaks about his teams like they're standing right next to him.

"Are you working tonight?" he says.

"Mos def."

"Despite the . . . decrepitude?"

I shove him off. "It's not like I'm running marathons or anything. Scan, receipt, repeat."

"I know. I know."

"Max and Antonia will be impressed with the injuries anyway. It's so fun to come in after a disaster. You're the battered war hero. You're famous."

"Brother, you think I don't know?" Jess raises his hands. "I can't eat. I'm famous already."

Will shrieks. We exchange looks.

"That which does not kill us makes us stronger," Jesse deadpans.

"Exactly. Exactly."

Self-improvement through adversity . . . it isn't bullshit. Exhibit A: my little brother. I can see every muscle in his stomach and shoulders.

He checks his watch. "I'm going to shower. Am I driving?"

I hold up my arm. "Well, I can't exactly, can I?"

Jesse laughs. "At least I get something out of this."

Jesse. This is not about you.

But I love the damn boy. So I let him go shower, then dump the rest of my oatmeal in the sink.

seven

"JO-NAH," NAOMI SING-SONGS.

I wave her away, pulling up my feet so I'm cross-legged on the hood of her station wagon. Jess clambers up next to me.

I point to the page in my hand. "Bleachers here?"

"Yeah. But make it cool and architectural."

I sketch in a bunch of triangles, I. M. Pei style. Good thing I'm left-handed.

Naomi says, "Smile for the camera, Jonah."

I look up and give her camera my biggest wired-shut smile.

She says, "Jesse."

He flips her off and she sticks out her tongue.

"Come on, Jess." She hits her zoom button. "Be cute."

He laughs, and she says, "There we go." She switches the camera to me. "What are you doing, Jonah?"

I draw a hard line. "I'm designing an ice rink for Jesse."

"My little future architect." She zooms in close to me, and I duck. "When are you gonna be famous, Jonah?"

"When my physics grades come up."

Jess says, "Add a supply closet there. But don't make it ugly."

"I never make anything ugly."

Naomi jumps out of the way to avoid being hit by an incoming car. It's heading for the space next to us. I catch sight of the driver and smile.

"I'm jumping," I say.

Jess says, "Don't."

"No, I am. Nom, get this filmed."

As soon as the car starts to brake, I leap from Naomi's hood and land squarely on the trunk of the other car with a huge thump. Charlotte shrieks inside and whips the door open. "What are you doing?"

Jesse is laughing so hard he's got his arms around his stomach to keep from splitting in half. Naomi giggles, and the camera shakes.

Charlotte runs over and shoves me in the chest. "You could have broken my car, you psychopath!"

I smile and tweak her on the nose. "Frankly, Charlotte, I don't give a—"

"Ugh, I hate it when you do that." She waves at the camera. "Hey, Naomi. Jesse."

His cheeks blush pink. Even my celibate brother isn't resistant to Charlotte's charms. Nobody is.

She leans over and kisses me on the cheek. "I'm late for Bio, and you're late for Calculus."

"All the more reason to hang out here with me."

She squints, examining me. "Naomi was right. You do look pretty awful."

"Thanks, babe."

She's not my girlfriend. I call everyone babe.

Seriously. Charlotte is not my girlfriend.

She touches my face. "You've got a black eye."

Naomi shuts off her camera in disgust. She likes me, and likes Charlotte, but isn't a fan of the two of us together.

I say, "Yeah, I painted it on this morning. Thought it made me look kind of badass."

Charlotte says, "Mission accomplished. What'd you use, makeup?"

"Yeah. Jesse's."

Jesse squawks, and Charlotte laughs. Naomi pulls her baseball cap down farther and rolls her eyes.

I continue. "He's a cross-dresser on Saturday nights. You didn't know? He goes to karaoke bars and struts around to ABBA. He's like six foot five in high heels."

Jesse shrugs and pulls his feet up on Naomi's fender. "It's true."

Charlotte lifts her finger toward my cheek. "So I could just rub this off—?"

I jerk away. "It's actually this kind of makeup that hurts when you touch it."

"Oh."

"Yeah. Jesse's into the S and M."

She winks at him. "I knew that kid was twisted."

"Yep. He's got a freaky soul under that allergic exterior."

She turns to him. "You don't really—"

He shakes his head apologetically.

I say, "Ha-ha, no. Although I should start telling people he does. He'd probably appreciate people recognizing him for something other than his immune system." I hand him what I've finished of his ice rink, and he looks it over, his smile widening.

Charlotte leans over and whispers in my ear. "My sister thinks he's cute."

"That's adorable. We'll have to do something about that."

Naomi stands on her tiptoes to be seen. "As precious

as this is, looks like I'm going to have to bail before I vomit."

Jess hops off Naomi's car and walks with her toward the building. "You're both going to be late," he calls to Charlotte and me.

I look at Charlotte and shrug one shoulder. "You want to be late?"

She rolls her eyes at me and hurries to catch up to Jesse and Naomi. I smile and follow her.

eight

"WHAT ABOUT YOUR NECK?" NAOMI SAYS, FLIPPING through her Google printouts.

I spin my combination. "I know. The plan still has a few kinks to work out."

"And skull?"

"Okay. So yeah, there are a couple I'm not real anxious to break." I open my locker and stuff eight pounds of physics homework into my backpack. My binder explodes and papers pour to the ground. "Shit. You want to help with this, Nom?"

She fixes her cap and doesn't bend down. "Look. I'm fine with taking some film of you fracturing a few fingers and toes, all right? Not so anxious to watch my best friend die for a prank."

Great. For Naomi it's a prank. For Jess it's an attention ploy. They really know how to personalize my actions. For themselves.

Marten Conway stops and touches my shoulder. "Jesus Christ, McNab. What the hell happened to you?"

I scoop the papers up in my good hand. "Tripped off Mount Everest."

"Yeah, clearly. You're just a little mess nowadays, aren't you?"

"I'm clumsy." I smile politely, hoping this will be enough to eschew him. I've got nothing against Marten, but this whole tragic hero thing can get tiring. Especially when it comes from everyone you know. All day.

"I've got to get to work," I tell Naomi as Marten saunters off, shaking his head at my state. "Can you drive me?"

She smiles and looks over my shoulder. "Ask your girlfriend."

I know who it is without turning around. I hear the clack of her red flats, and my jaw hurts from trying not to smile.

But ritual is ritual. I raise my voice and say, "Charlotte is not my girlfriend."

"That is so mean." Charlotte elbows me in the back. "I would never say you weren't my girlfriend."

I turn around. "Hello, not-girlfriend."

"Hey, not-boyfriend. Need help?" She scoops my papers off the ground. What an angel.

"Thanks, babe."

She hands me a pile of shit and I cram it in my backpack. I turn to Naomi. "I still need that ride."

"Get Jesse."

"He's in practice until three thirty. And I've got a shift at three."

"Call your mom."

"Busy with Will."

"Then ask your girlfriend."

I shrug my shoulders to Charlotte, wearing my hopeful face.

She smiles and tips her ponytail over her shoulder. "Yeah, I can take you. Meetcha at my car?"

"Okay."

Charlotte walks away, and I laugh at Naomi. "You thought she'd say no."

"Fuck yeah, I did. Watch, she's going to come in pregnant tomorrow. And you're gonna be sweaty, and saying, 'Oh, man,' over and over again."

"Relax, you. It's a ride home, not a naked romp.

You're like a fucking Desperate Housewife sometimes."

She scrunches her mousy little face. "That 'fucking' was so out of place."

"Yeah, well, I've got fucking-rollover minutes. I'm full to burst, here. I can't cuss at home, and I can't cuss in front of Charlotte."

"Sure. You won't cuss in front of her, but you'll bone her till she bleeds."

"She's a virgin. They bleed, Nom. Not that you'd know."

"Fuck off."

"We don't bone."

"You think about it."

"Of course I think about it." I blow air inside my wrist cast to quell an itch. "If I didn't think about it, I'd need to be taken in for hormone testing."

"You disgust me," she says, and stomps away in those ugly-ass combat boots.

My Jesse-sense is tingling. Half the time it's bullshit—okay, more than half the time—but I still don't like to take chances. I take out my cell phone and hit 2 to speed dial him.

He doesn't answer. I call back and he gets it on the second ring. "Hello?"

He's out of breath, and his voice is muffled through half his hockey gear.

"What up, brother?" I say.

"I'm in practice, Jo."

"Oh, right." And I hang up. He's fine.

Charlotte leans against her car. The iris she's stuck into the base of her ponytail droops a little to the side.

Every day, she puts a fresh real flower in her hair. She wears her beauty like I wear my casts.

"Pop in," she says, sliding into the driver's seat.

I sit down beside her and prop my backpack on my lap. Some of the Tweety Bird trinkets and sheets of balled-up paper shower down from her dashboard onto me, but I don't mind. "Thanks for this, babe."

"No problem. Consider it thanks for not actually destroying my car this morning."

I smile. "That was hilarious."

"Hilariously scary. I thought I'd been hit by a meteor." She starts the car. "Guess you can't drive with the cast, yeah?"

"Well, I can. I just can't steer so well."

"Oh."

"But I can drive, you know. On sidewalks and over pedestrians and stuff."

She giggles, her dark pink lips drawing together over her teeth. We've bantered like this since sophomore year and she still always breaks.

But every time she holds out for longer and longer.

We didn't start bantering exclusively until this September.

"So," she says, and brushes a curl behind her ear. "So what really happened?"

"Oh, you mean—" I gesture over my wrecked body.

"Yeah."

"Skateboard. Trying out this tricky jump with Naomi and—bam."

Technically, none of this is a lie.

"Ouch."

"Uh-huh."

"How many bones have you broken now?"

"Oh, I don't know."

Ha, ha.

"It's got to be, like, ten," she says.

Puh.

"Man." She flicks her eyes to me behind her fancy glasses. "You and your brother are just little medical disasters, aren't you?" She frowns. "Or was that a faux pas?"

I smile to show her it's okay and sit back in the car seat. "Nah. He's way more disastrous than I am."

"You think?"

"But, I mean . . . he's been okay. He hasn't had an ER visit this whole month."

"And you're going on how long?"

"Okay, like twenty hours. Point taken. But it's not the same."

"My sister thinks he's amazing." Charlotte glides into the left lane.

"You know his middle name's James," I say.

"Seriously?"

"Uh-huh. Jesse James McNab."

"That's wicked."

"Yeah. My parents used to like outlaws. Now they're just middle Americans," I stretch. "How old's your sister?"

"Fourteen. Freshman."

"Jess is sixteen."

"I know. But he's . . . relatively innocent, isn't he?"

Well, sure. He can't exactly go mouth-to-mouth. At least not with girls who eat. I should set him up with a nice anorexic.

"She'd take care of him," Charlotte says.

"I know she would. I'm just not sure if what he really needs is another set of hands trying to take care of him. He gets annoyed enough with me sometimes, and he needs me."

"She likes him, Jonah."

"All right. I'll talk to him."

"So," she says. "My choral director gave me this huge

solo at our next concert." We're getting close to work, now. Damn.

I smile at her. "That's awesome."

"Right, right, yeah. But it's the *alto* solo. He gave me the alto solo. And I'm a soprano."

"Oh." Yeah, I'm not following this at all, but *God* I could watch Charlotte complain for hours.

She says, "So now I'm at this weird impasse. 'Cause if I remind him, *Hey, I've been a soprano since I was in diapers,* I lose the solo, right?"

"Oh, no, don't do that." Possibly the only thing better than listening to Charlotte complain is listening to her sing. And also listening to those little moaning noises she makes when we kiss, like she's eating chocolate cake. . . .

Oh, she's still talking. ". . . keep it, I'll probably sound awful trying to sing in a vocal range I usually don't touch with a ten-foot pole."

"I really don't think you sounding awful is within the realm of possibility."

"These are ill-timed compliments, Jonah."

"Oh, really?"

"Yes! You are supposed to be helping me plot my next move, not making me blush. Tsk tsk."

"You're not blushing."

She is smiling, though. "Clearly I stay on task better

than you do." She pulls up to the curb. "What time are you off? We can continue our brainstorming. I'm thinking poisoning my choir director might be the best solution?"

"Don't get off until seven, sadly."

"Do you need a ride home?"

"Nah. Jesse'll pick me up."

She tilts her head to the side. "So can you kiss me with your jaw like that?"

I do the best I can.

The door jangles as I nudge it open. Max and Antonia are behind the counters, feet on the sensors that make sure no one runs away with the DVDs. Antonia tosses gummi worms into the air and catches them in her mouth three at a time. No one eats gummi worms like Antonia.

"Hey."

They turn around and freeze. "Holy mackerel," Max says. "What tree did you fall out of?"

Antonia coughs and scoots her ass off her knee-length blond hair. "Ugly tree, clearly."

I sign in. "Thanks, Toni."

"Shit, give him some java, Max. He's going to need it. Seriously, what happened?"

I catch the bag of coffee beans Max hurls over. "Skateboard accident. I'm fine."

"What'd you break?"

"Two ribs, wrist, jaw." I take out two coffee beans and swallow them like pills. The bitterness burns the hardware in my mouth.

Antonia decapitates a gummi worm. "You break more bones than anyone I've ever seen."

"Thank you."

"That's not a compliment, Jonah."

That's what you think.

"How long are you in the cast?" Max asks.

"Probably, like, three weeks. So, enough. What have you guys been up to?"

Max clears his throat and Antonia straightens her little string vest.

"Oh." I clear my throat. "Never mind."

No one comes to the store this early, so Antonia and Max use it as a personal kissing booth when I'm not around. It would be irritating if they both weren't so damn cute. They're like Martians.

"Come on." Antonia dives into the candy display, her pale lower legs flailing about like fish from her denim skirt. "I was just about to dig into the malted milk balls."

I step behind the counter and plop down beside the cash register. "So you guys remember Charlotte?"

Max and Antonia go to this hippie private school

down the street. All they know of real life is what I tell them. They're my science experiment.

Antonia's eyes light up. "She's the one with the puff-paint flowers on her license plate," she chimes.

"Right."

Max gestures big boobs with his hands. Antonia throws a malt ball at him.

"So all's not right in wonderland?" Antonia licks chocolate off her fingers.

"It's not that. She's got this little sister she wants to set up with Jesse."

Max looks up from the late returns. "Isn't Jesse, like, dying of AIDS?"

Antonia's mouth drops open. "Max!"

"He does not have AIDS," I say.

Max hands *Fight Club* to Antonia. "Well, he's dying of something, isn't he?"

"Food allergies," I say. "And he's not dying. But if he dates Charlotte's little sister, isn't that practically incest?"

Antonia says, "I thought you and Charlotte *weren't dating*."

"We're not. Hush."

"Then it's not incest." Max stamps two movies. "It's merely two brothers enjoying the company of two girls who happen to be related."

"Yeah, but . . . enjoying to what extent?"

"Ew." Antonia picks up a few movies and shoves them under her arm. "Come on. I'm bored of dissecting Jonah's love life."

"Not-love life," I correct.

She rolls her head around. "Whatever. I'm going to the back. Let's go have a screening." She grabs Max's hand. "Coming, Jonah?"

I shake my head. "I'll watch the register."

"Sure?"

"Yeah. Who knows. Someone might come."

I spend almost an hour at the register trying not to think about Jesse and Mini-Charlotte and trying not to listen to Antonia and Max make slurping noises. Eventually, customers start to trickle in, and I go through the motions.

See, the whole job is fucking worthless. I come here for a few hours after school a few days a week and slog through movie advice and cash-register Olympics like I actually know anything. At least it gets me away from my family for a little while. But I wish I were with Charlotte.

At about four thirty, I point a girl toward the documentaries and rescue my ringing phone from my pocket.

"Can you come home?" Jesse says. "There's milk everywhere and I'm throwing up."

"Seriously?"

"Yeah. I've thrown up four times in the past, like, twenty minutes. Can you get home?"

"Where the hell is Mom?"

"Took Will to the doctor. Jonah, seriously. I'm sitting outside so I don't have to smell it, and it's fucking cold."

"Did you take Benadryl?"

"Yeah. It stayed down for a good thirty seconds."

This is as close as Jesse ever gets to angry, and I think he's pissed-off more seriously than he's sick. That's easier to deal with, at least, though I still feel bad for the kid. "I can get out of the shift if you need me," I say, "but do you think you could pick me up? I don't have a ride out of here."

He makes exasperated-disbelieving noises.

I say, "It'd probably do you good to get away from the house."

He coughs and says, "I'm going to throw up again."

"All right," I relent worthlessly, as his footsteps rush away from the phone. "I'll get home."

I finish checking out the last customer and venture into the back for Max and Antonia. They scoot away from each other as soon as I open the door, like they're afraid their cuddling will bruise my eyes.

I say, "So you know my brother who's dying of AIDS?"

Max cleans his glasses on his shirt. "Yeah."

"Yeah, well, he's having, like, an AIDS attack. So I need to get home."

He looks at me critically. "Everything okay?"

"He'll be fine. But he's home alone and I need to get to him. So—"

He waves his hand. "Take the shift off. Antonia and I can handle."

"That's not it. I sort of need a ride."

He chews his cheek, studying me, then turns to Antonia and speaks to her in some sort of romantic hippie language. She nods, pulls her hair over her shoulder, and traipses out to the front desk.

"I'll drive you home," Max says, shoving his arms through the sleeves of his denim jacket.

"Thanks, man. I appreciate it."

He shrugs.

Max's van has a bench seat at the front and endless empty space in the back. I climb in and sling my backpack onto the dirty floor. He starts the engine. His feet barely reach the pedals. I push back against the headrest like I'm on one of those carnival rides and the floor's about to drop out. I don't know how to tell him to drive faster without sounding like a nervous wreck. So I just wait until he gets to my house, then smile and thank him and shake his hand.

"Jesse?"

He's throwing up. I hear it through the bathroom door. My stomach squeezes, but it's hard to be too squeamish when you've got a brother who throws up as much as he does.

I lean against the door. "How you feeling?"

He runs the tap, probably to drown out the noise.

I say, "How is there anything left in your stomach?"

He shouts, "Guess I've been saving up!"

"I'm going to clean."

He retches.

"You okay? You didn't touch any of it, did you?"

"If I touched it, I wouldn't be breathing."

Good point. The boy's unbelievably allergic to milk. It's dramatic even for him.

The kitchen is a wreck. The refrigerator's propped open—great—and one of Will's overturned bottles drips onto the floor. There's a saucepan full of milk on a burner that's still hot.

"Solved the mystery," I yell to Jesse. "There's milk on the stove in here."

He steps out of the bathroom, wiping his mouth on the back of his hand. "Great." He's covered in pink nickel-size spots—calamine lotion over the hives.

I make my responsible older-brother face. "Go into

the living room and lie down, all right? I'll clean up in here."

I take the pan off the stove and rinse it in the sink, watching all the milk run down the drain. I put the bottle in the refrigerator, close the refrigerator, and give the countertops and floor a good scrub. Wash my hands. Open all the windows. The October wind stings the back of my throat.

"It's going to get cold in here," I tell him as I flop down on the couch beside him. "I'm airing the kitchen out."

He pulls the quilt off the back of the couch and drapes it over us.

"It's kind of a problem that you get this sick just from the smell," I say.

"I know."

"And I know food challenges suck, but you've got to get more tolerant than this."

Jess used to do challenges where he had to eat tiny bits—like, *really* tiny bits—of something he's allergic to every day. The point is that your body deals. Starts to accept it. And then you eat a little more, then a little more. Just building up. Immune system overcomes the challenge.

But Jess always ended up getting sick as hell whenever he was in a challenge, and a few years ago he said he wouldn't do them anymore.

He rolls his eyes and lies down, his head next to my knee.

I shove my hand in his hair and turn on the TV to some game show. "Let me know if you get bad, okay?"

He says, "Okay."

The show's so boring that Jess falls asleep within minutes. And I'm only half-conscious when Mom turns the key in the lock and slogs in, screaming baby on her hip.

Jess groans and throws a pillow over his head.

"Want to take the noise somewhere else?" I say. "He's in the middle of a reaction."

"Gosh, really?" She hovers over him, mothering to the best of her ability when she's not allowed to touch him. "What happened?"

I hold the pillow over his head so he'll stay asleep. "You left milk on the stove, is what happened."

She touches her forehead with her non–baby-wielding hand. "I didn't."

"Yeah, you did. Which is irresponsible enough considering the whole fire hazard thing, but you might as well have left frickin' cyanide boiling—"

"Jonah, I don't need a lecture."

I shut up.

She says, "Are you going to be okay, Jesse?"

He nods and the pillow shakes. "What'd the doctor say?"

She walks back and forth with Will, bouncing him with her shoulder. "He doesn't know. He said it could still be colic, that sometimes it'll last this long." She pauses, hand in her hair. "I'll bring Will upstairs and give him a bath, okay?" She directs this to me.

I say, "Okay."

Jesse falls back asleep, snoring through his congestion, and I'm left with this awful feeling in my mouth, like I've been swallowing carpet. I'd get up and drink something, or walk around, if it weren't so damn cold and I didn't have a responsibility to watch Jesse. I need to just shut up and be here for him.

I squeeze my eyes shut and try to distract myself.

So. Distraction. *How about another bone, Jonah?*

My mouth twitches up.

How about tomorrow?

nine

WHEN I WAKE UP AT 5:57 THE NEXT MORNING AND hear the squeak-squeak of Jesse on the rowing machine, I trudge downstairs and find Mom eating toast at the kitchen table, baby tucked under her arm.

"Hi."

Her mouth's full, so she waves. I rescue Will. He's turning purple from crying so hard.

When you hold him close enough to your ear, it's impossible to think.

Sort of nice.

"I wanted to talk to you," Mom says.

What is it about that sentence that makes your stomach curl up?

She pats the table across from her. Will's getting as close as he ever is to quiet, just doing his pissed-off whine. I sit down and try to concentrate on Jesse's rowing and Will's whimpers instead of her.

"I haven't really gotten to speak with you since the accident," she says. "How're the breaks feeling?"

"Okay. I took some aspirin."

"Good." She rakes her hair back in one hand. "Been praying?"

Shit. "Yeah, Mom."

She sighs and takes my hand. "We feel guilty about this, Jonah."

I wonder if it's only religious parents who always tell you how they feel. And I wonder if it's only terrible children who don't want to hear it.

"Why?" I say. "I'm just clumsy."

She lays her fingertips over her mouth. "If there's something going on—"

"Nothing's going on."

Will's loud again, and Mom has to shout. "You know your dad and I love you very—"

"I know, Mom. Thanks." I'm at a loss for what this had to do with anything. I stand up and cradle Will over to the sink, start sponging the counter.

Quietly, Mom says, "You know what he does, though.

He belittles you. He pits you and Jesse against each other."

"Stop it. I could never be against Jesse." Even if I wanted to be.

She looks down and traces the woodwork on the table. "Well . . . look, darling, could you talk to him, then?"

"What?"

"Talk to Dad. Tell him you're okay, that you know our family's okay. That you're keeping the family in mind." Her lips fold into an envelope. "That's all I mean."

"You tell him. I'm not getting involved in your issues."

"Jonah."

"No. You handle Dad, and I handle Jesse. Those are the rules."

We've never said this out loud, but it's become clear over the years that we've made an agreement. It worked out fine until Will was born. Now we're outnumbered.

She scrapes her toast. "Your father doesn't listen to me."

"Don't do this. I'm not your therapist. Hire a marriage counselor. Use his money. This isn't about me."

"Of course it is."

I set Will on the counter and pour orange juice. "I've got to get ready for school."

"Stop it, Jonah."

"Look," I say. "I don't want to argue about this. I'm fine. Everything's fine. I just fell off my skateboard. It happens. People fall all the time."

"People don't usually *break* things."

"I wasn't wearing the pads. I'm a reckless teenager. Ground me. But stop making this some big issue." I finish the orange juice. Forget oatmeal. I wash the baby-spit off my hands, shake out Jesse's pills, and head downstairs with a Coke.

He's resting on the edge of the rowing machine, his elbows on his knees.

"Good set?" I ask.

He nods. "Half hour. No stopping."

"You're a force, brother."

He coughs. "Mom pissed?"

"Kind of. It'll be good for her. She needs some cardiac exercise." I hand him the pills. "She's fine."

"I know." Jesse dry-swallows the pills. "She's always fine."

ten

BEFORE CALC, I MAKE OUT WITH CHARLOTTE BEHIND
the gym.

"Why, not-boyfriend," she whispers, running her lips
down my neck. "This is so naughty."

I say, "Shh."

She takes off my army hat and plunks it onto her
head. It completely covers her bun and way-pierced ears.

"I have to go," I say.

"Nooo."

I pull her close. She's twenty degrees warmer than I
am, and her winter-skin's dry and her breath is wet. Not-
dating leaves so much room for lust.

"You have study hall," I say into her mouth.

She giggles. "Right. I'm supposed to be learning. Supposed to be getting"—she licks my teeth—"educated."

"Ow."

She pulls back. "I'm sorry. Did I hurt your mouth?"

Like kerosene. "A little."

"I'm sorry."

"You said that already. It's okay."

"It's probably a little too early in the recovery process for making out."

"It's okay, really." Really.

She kisses the side of my jaw, gently, then moves her mouth down to the top of my chest. I look down at the top of my cap, the fold of fabric where her head doesn't fill all the space. Her mouth is so warm, like a splash of hot water every time we make contact.

"Beautiful," I say.

"Hmm?"

"You. You're beautiful."

She stops kissing and wraps her arms around my waist, her forehead against my broken ribs. "That's a suspiciously boyfriend-type remark."

"No way."

"Way."

"Hush, you." I push my hand under her shirt. I'm aware that, in a few hours, I'll have no good hands left.

This might be my only opportunity to touch her for a long time.

She moans and arches her back into my hand. "Love you."

"Aw, man, Charlotte. Don't."

She doesn't get mad, just pushes away from me, fingers in my belt loops. "I have to go," she says.

"Noooo." I laugh. "I changed my mind. Stay."

Her eyelashes flutter like hundreds of butterflies. "But I do have to go. I promised Naomi I'd help her with Bio."

"Blow her off."

"I can't."

"Sure you can. I do it all the time."

She huffs and messes with her bun, rearranging the daisy so it's visible around her curls and my hat. "Are we hanging out after school?"

Crap. I've got to break tonight.

But I can give her a few hours first. Maybe finish what I started?

It's delirious thinking, but it's the only kind of thinking I can manage when I'm with Charlotte.

I say, "Absolutely."

We kiss, and I taste her. I don't love her—I can only muster that for Jess and occasionally Will, and when you claim "love" about a girl it's stupid and ephemeral and everyone knows it. It's like a big joke.

Plus, she's not my girlfriend.

No girlfriend could ever be this good.

eleven

MY PHONE JINGLES AS I HEAD TO CHARLOTTE'S car after school. It's Jesse, and he's not feeling well.

I say, "Not feeling well or feeling seriously awful?"

"Not feeling well. I think I'm okay."

"Breathe."

He does, and I listen, and he sounds fine. But how sure can you be over a cell phone?

He says, "It's nothing major. Don't freak out on me. Probably just the pollen."

It's practically November. "Jesse."

"Look, I'm honestly fine. I'll call if it gets bad. I just wanted to tell you I'm skipping practice and going home."

"You're skipping practice."

"Don't make this a big deal."

I close my eyes because it's too hard to look at Charlotte on the edge of her car, her curves just begging for me to come and put my hands on them. "Do you need me to come home?"

"No. No no no. You have plans with Charlotte, right?"

"Yeah."

"Don't break those. Mom will watch me."

Yeah, okay. "I won't be gone too long. Stay away from the baby."

"I know, Jonah. God."

"And call in half an hour. No matter what."

"Okay."

I hang up and climb into Charlotte's passenger seat. "Sorry. Duty called."

"Duty?"

"Duty, thy name is Jesse."

"Right." She starts the car and honks her horn until the pack of sophomores gets away from her back bumper. "He all right?"

"Yeah, I don't know. It's hard to tell. He said he wasn't feeling well, and you never know what that means."

"Do you need to go home?"

"No, he'll be fine."

"You sure?" She looks at me. "I know how you are with him. If you want to go home, it's okay."

I shake my head. "I don't want to be home. I want to be with my not-girlfriend."

She slides on her sunglasses and hits the gas.

After-school trips with Charlotte mean trailing her through her house visits. She's a pet-sitter, and every day she's got about a thousand neglected animals to feed and pet and bathe. It's kind of tedious, but it's with Charlotte. And I don't usually get to spend time around animals, so . . .

The first house is one I've visited before; it's brown brick and all the furniture is plush. I sit on the couch and pet one of the Siamese while Charlotte fills the water bowls.

The clock hits three o'clock and makes a noise like a wind chime.

"Going away for Christmas?" she asks, random.

"Like always. Somewhere cold and dry. My entire life is about what's good for lungs."

"So I know it's early to talk about, but my parents wanted me to invite you to help decorate our tree. If you want."

"That's sweet. But kind of relationshipy for me, babe."

She comes in to the living room, dusting her hands

on her jeans. "I just figured you're not much used to Christmas trees."

"Nah, not really. I probably had one my first Christmas." I shrug. "Before Jess was born."

We've got a big aluminum one, but I've seen Naomi's trees, so I can't pretend it's the same. It's okay, though.

Charlotte sits on my lap and holds the cat.

Later we walk with these three Pomeranians around the block and Charlotte stops, ties the leashes to a lamppost, and we kiss. Gently.

"Do you think—" I say, going for her zipper.

She holds my hand. "Shh."

"But—"

My phone rings. Shit. I think I was actually getting somewhere.

It's Jesse and screaming Will. "I'm totally fine," Jess says.

Over the phone, Will's especially strangled and grainy. I wince. Nothing like a baby to scare an erection away.

I say, "Totally?"

"Yeah. I feel great. I was an idiot to skip practice."

I hang up and stare at Charlotte. She shrugs and reclaims the leashes.

When I get home, I change clothes before Jess can sneeze at me.

"Basketball?" he asks.

"All right."

I last about five minutes against him, and he keeps going and going like a boy possessed.

twelve

NAOMI PULLS UP AT AROUND SEVEN. I'M CRASHED on the lawn, watching Jess take practice shots in the dark. I see the glint of a six-pack in her backseat.

She swings out of the car and leans against the door. The sleeves of my sweatshirt she's stolen cover her fingers. "Hey, Jess."

He throws her the basketball. She catches it in her tiny hands and throws it back.

"Ready to go?" she says. "Jesus, I can hear the baby from here."

"Want to see him?"

"Not at all."

Jess wrinkles his forehead, dribbling the ball between his legs. "Where are you going?"

I wave my good hand in his face. "Work to do."

He holds the ball. "You're kidding."

I shrug.

"Jonah, don't. Shit, man. Mom and Dad are going to freak out."

"I know they will. I'll make sure you're out of the room first."

"You." Jess nods at Naomi. "You let him do this?"

She shrugs and bites her knuckle. "What am I supposed to do? It's his body. He can do what he wants."

I tilt my head at Jesse.

"Don't do this now," he says.

"What, like there's going to be a better time than now?"

"You shouldn't do this *anytime*, idiot."

I glance toward the house. "Hush up, all right? Mom's going to hear you."

He exhales. "I have half a mind to tell them what you're doing."

"Yeah, good thing that other half is smart enough to keep your damn mouth shut. Look. I'll be fine. So just be a good little brother and keep quiet for Mom and Dad, okay?"

He says, "This is the last one I'm letting you do."

"I'll call in about an hour, all right?"

I clamber into Naomi's car and put my feet on the dashboard. The bend hurts my ribs, but it's worth it. "Just drive away, okay? I don't want to look at him."

She listens, but when we're halfway out of the neighborhood, she says, "You're hurting him."

My ears are free of baby wail. "I am. Not. Hurting him."

She knows enough to shut up.

We park behind the old fire station. Naomi wants me to get really drunk, but I know they'll do a blood-alcohol check at the hospital and I don't want to get in trouble. So we take just one beer each and sip while we sit on the hood of her car. Our feet dangle over the windows.

"You scared?" she asks.

I nod. "This one's going to hurt."

"At least it'll be over quick. And it'll definitely look like an accident."

"How bad is it going to be?"

"Well, it's going to hurt, Jonah. It'll be bloody."

I exhale. "Shit."

"You'll be fine."

"It's not going to be the best video. Who the hell wants to watch some idiot break his hand in a car door?"

She squirms inside my sweatshirt. "Yeah, but the video's not the point, is it?"

Of course it's not, but I didn't think she knew this.

"All right, Jo." She drains the remains of her beer and clonks the empty can onto the hood. "You ready?"

"Ready as I'll ever be, I guess."

"That's the spirit." She sets the camera up on the tripod and does all her tech-girl shit, because I guess the video still matters a little bit.

I hop down and open the driver's side door. "Shit," I breathe.

"It's going to be fine." She comes back and places her hand on my shoulder. "Put your hand in."

I take one last look at my unbroken, imperfect hand and place it in the seam between the door and its frame. I wiggle my fingers.

"Now?" Naomi says, poised on the handle.

"No. Not yet."

"Jonah."

"Just wait a second."

I puff air in and out of my mouth, trying to build up some kind of courage. I can do this. It's worth it. *You'll be better because of it, Jonah.* I breathe.

"Now?" she says.

My cell phone starts vibrating. "Hold on." I pull my

phone out of my pocket. NEW TEXT MESSAGE. I swallow. "It's from Mom."

Text messages from Mom are always the same thing. It's always Jesse.

I shouldn't have left. Shit. My chest starts jumping.

Naomi says, "Does she want you home?"

I flip it open to read the text message.

JESSE 911

Yeah. And I can't breathe anymore.

Jesse.

I left him at home with Mom and the dirty house and the baby vomit and he had hives when I left, he had hives and I *left him alone.*

Naomi says, "Does she need you to pick up some baby food for your perfect family—"

"Naomi, shut up."

She bristles. "What?"

"It's Jesse."

I hear her pause, and when she talks she sounds like a little girl. "Is he okay?"

I look up. "When I say, 'It's Jesse' in that voice, is he ever okay?"

"God, Jonah, I'm—"

"Shit!" I yell, and slap my hands up to my eyes. The cast scrapes me—goddamn cast—so I slam it against the firehouse wall. "Fuck!" I yell, pounding my arm on the brick, punching it, hitting it, asking it why the hell I'm here and not with my brother. "Fuck fuck shit shit shit shit shit! He's in the hospital, Naomi!"

"He'll be okay."

My throat hurts so badly and pain explodes from my broken wrist down to my fingertips, but I should have been there I should have been there—

"Jonah. Jonah." She grabs me and wraps her arms around me, her chest against the small of my back. "Stop it."

I feel her deep breathing against me and it reminds me that this is real. That I'm really here and really this upset, and I really screwed up this badly.

"He could die," I say.

She turns me around and reaches up to my face. Her hands are so cold against my skin. "He didn't die. Now stop crying."

I do, but I don't feel any better. My nose is running all over my face.

"Get in the car," she says. "I'll take you to the hospital and you can see him. Jesse's going to be fine. He's always fine."

Of course he's always fine. If he ever wasn't fine, this would all be over. He wouldn't have any more opportunities to get sick. Any more near-scrapes.

They can't all be near-scrapes.

She guides me to the car and buckles the seatbelt over my lap. "Get your cell phone out and call your mom. Find out what's going on."

"I can't."

"Jonah."

"Just shut the fuck up, Naomi!"

She turns the key in the ignition and doesn't talk anymore. I put my good hand and my throbbing cast over my face.

He will be fine.

If he wasn't fine, the message would have said JESSE MORGUE.

911 just means they called an ambulance.

It just means he had a bad reaction.

What did he eat? I try a mental inventory. Apple at breakfast. Protein shake. Rice cake. Coke. Another protein shake.

I say, "What have you eaten today?"

She glances up from the road. "What?"

"What was on your hands when you touched his basketball?"

"Nothing." She fixes her cap. "I had pizza, like, three hours ago."

I throw my hands up.

"Three hours ago, Jonah! That is so far-fetched. He could have touched anything! Your Mom's boobs are leaking all over the house."

"You *know* you have to be careful—"

"I was careful! I'm always careful with him. Jesus Christ! I was there for two minutes. You really think he got this from *me?*"

"What are you saying?"

"He already wasn't feeling well. And you were with Charlotte and all the cats—"

"I changed my clothes!" My ribs feel like they're getting punched. "This is not my—"

"I'm sorry, I'm sorry." She exhales, shaking her head. "I'm not saying anything."

She grew up with Jesse just like I did, and I know this is hard for her, but it'd be easier to honor that if she'd appreciate it's hard for me, too. That I'm not just pointing fingers here. That I'm trying to solve something. That I'm trying to keep my goddamn brother alive, every single fucking day.

"God." I put my head back. "God, I hate the hospital."

She says, "Call your mom."

I give up and take out my cell phone.

She's all breathless. "Hello?"

"What happened?"

I hear all that stomach-throbbing ambulance noise,

and I think I'm going to puke on Naomi's grody uphol-stery. "We don't know," she says. "He took his EpiPen and it looks like one dose is going to be enough."

Sometimes we have to keep hitting him and hitting him with epinephrine to keep him conscious. . . . It's pretty awful. He'll be jumpy for days after that.

"Did you see him have anything, Jonah?"

She's asking me if I poisoned him.

"No. He didn't have anything when I was with him."

I ask it right back.

She just makes all these heartbroken noises. I'm mak-ing a habit of underestimating how hard this is for any-one but me and Jesse.

"Can I talk to him?" I say.

"No, honey, he can't talk right now."

I wait for Jesse to snatch the phone, but he doesn't. I say, "Is Dad there?"

"No, he's home with the baby. Trying to get a sitter so he can come down here. We're at the hospital now, Jonah. Are you on your way?"

"Yeah. We'll be there soon." I look at Naomi, who nods and leans on the gas.

In ten minutes, the gray building rises in front of us like a sick beacon. I'm mocked by the pictures of happy children on the direction signs.

"Go to the south lot," I say. "It's never crowded."

We walk into the parking garage and take the elevator to the ER entrance. I have to stop when we get inside because I'm shaking too hard.

"Everything's going to be fine," Naomi says, and I wish she'd shut up because it's not like this will ever stop.

She holds the top of my arms and lets me tremble. People flow around me, respectfully. People who understand, or feel like they should.

He has a lot of reactions. I don't usually freak out this badly.

Naomi eventually nudges me up to the ER front desk. I weave through the bleeding old women and hacking children on benches and find the receptionist behind heaps of clipboards. "I'm looking for Jesse McNab. Probably got here by ambulance. He'd still be on the floor."

She checks a sheet of paper in front of her. "Oh, is he the teenager? The cute teenager with anaphylaxis?"

I bite my top lip to keep it still. "Yeah."

"Betty?" She cranes her head back to some hospital nether region. "Where'd the ambulance teenager go?"

"109," says some disembodied voice.

"He's in 109," the volunteer repeats. "Down the hall. Odd numbers are on the right."

For some reason I keep staring at her and won't move

away from the desk. She clears her throat, but Naomi has to grab my arm before I'll leave.

We walk down the hall, pass eight curtained doors. I hear babies crying and bones being set. A hollow-eyed nurse wheels a cart of vomit basins. It's like this is hell, and it's been created just for me and Naomi and Jesse. And Mom, I guess.

When I get to 109, Naomi says, "Look, I'll leave."

"You don't have to." *He's yours, too.*

"Yeah, I do. Listen, I'll go to your house and watch Will, okay? Then your dad can get down here."

"Nom, you don't have to."

"It's okay, really."

We shuffle our feet against the linoleum. Part of me is dying for her to go so I can see Jesse, and part wants to grab her and hold on to her so I won't have to go into his room.

I swallow. "Um . . . call Charlotte, all right? Let her know."

"Sure." She gives me a tight-lipped smile. "Give him . . . you know, something from me, all right?"

I watch her go, drowning in that damn sweatshirt.

All right.

I push open the curtain, and there's Jesse.

He's in the bed, curled up, his swollen eyes closed.

Hives cover his arms, and he's got an IV in the back of his hand and an oxygen mask over his nose and mouth.

Mom is talking to the doctor, saying, "I know, I know," over and over. She looks up and says, "Jonah." Then she ignores me, because there's really not much more to say to me.

The doctor doesn't look at me. Probably assumes I'm unimportant.

"Still no idea what happened?" I ask.

She shakes her head.

It's usually this way. Usually, we do all we fucking think we can and something gets through to Jesse, and we never know what. Or how. Or what we can do to fix him.

The doctors always tell Mom the same thing this one's telling her now. Take this precaution. That precaution. Wean the baby. Cross-contamination. Do this to build his tolerance—he should not still be so sensitive. Consider home-schooling him. Consider a special school for him. Consider anything but a real life for him. Do anything but treat him like a real boy.

I scoot the chair closer to the bed and kneel next to him. "Hey. You up?"

He nods and opens his eyes. My stomach swoops like a Ferris wheel.

"How do you feel, brother?" I say.

He shrugs and takes the mask off. "Kind of hard to breathe still. Shit, what happened to your hand?"

I look down.

"No, the other one."

Oh. My cast has cracked open at the hand, and there's blood leaking out by the fingers. *Crap.*

"Don't worry about that," I tell him.

"Man—"

"Shh." I glance up at Mom, deep in conversation with the doctor. "I didn't do it on purpose. I freaked out and punched the wall."

He sighs. He's still wheezing.

"It's going to be okay," I say.

He winces. He hates that too.

"Sorry."

"Don't get inspirational speaker on me, Jonah."

"What do you want me to do?"

He crawls his hand out from under the covers. I lay my cast in my lap and reach out my other hand. My fingers touch his IV.

"I know I know I know," Mom says.

I squeeze Jess's hand.

thirteen

WITHIN A FEW HOURS WE'RE ALL BACK AT HOME. Jesse's still swollen and totally pissy and ends up collapsing on the couch, bitching at everyone who walks by. "It's midnight. I have school tomorrow," he whines whenever we wake him up to check if he's breathing.

I've got a new unbroken cast that covers my new broken hand. Metacarpal fracture. + 1 broken hand = 19.

Pretty damn lucky, hmm?

Naomi refuses money from my dad and gives me a wink on the way out. She squeezes Jesse's shoulder too, and I hope she washed her hands first.

Now Dad and I are silent in the kitchen.

"He's asleep," Mom says, walking in from the living room.

Dad hands me a bag of ice. "Good." He was only at the hospital for an hour or so, so he still has the sports-jacket-and-tie aura of real life. Mom and I, on the other hand, both look around the kitchen like we haven't seen it in years.

She slumps down at the table.

"We've got to do something," Dad says. He places his hand on the back of my neck. "He cannot keep having these attacks."

Mom's sweaty hair clings to her hands. "He's been better lately."

"Better is not nine trips to the hospital a year, Cara."

"Eleven," I mumble.

Mom hardens her eyes at Dad. "We shouldn't discuss this in front of Jonah. Can we think about what the Reverend said?"

I shrug.

Dad says, "Look, he's always better when we're both home. Maybe I should drop some hours. See if I can spend more time with him."

Mom scratches like Jesse. "You make it sound psychological."

"I don't. But the better he's watched—"

"I watch him just fine," Mom says.

I say, "I do too."

Dad raises his hands. "The fact of the matter is I had a sister like Jesse. I know what it takes to raise this type of kid."

Dad's sister died when she was eighteen. Bee sting.

"He's not a type," I say.

Dad ignores me. "Look." He turns back to Mom. "There are schools for kids like him. Even peanut-free would be a relief."

I say, "No one eats peanuts around him at school. They're not idiots."

Mom sighs. "Jesse wants to be with Jonah."

"If Jonah could take care of him—"

"Paul!"

I whisper, "It's okay."

We're quiet for a damn long time.

It's sort of against the rules to imply that I don't watch Jesse well enough.

Though everyone knows it anyway.

"All right," I say, when I get my voice back. "This is not a tragedy. Jesse doesn't need to change his life. We just need to keep the house cleaner. Just because—"

"Just because you're breaking bones every two minutes, Jonah?" Dad throws his hands in the air. "Yeah, I'll admit that's weighing on my mind."

Will's screaming shoots from his room to the kitchen. I picture him lying in his crib, his little hands in fists.

I tell Dad, "Stop. That has nothing to do with Jesse." I should just leave. But this would get a thousand times uglier if it were just between the two of them.

Dad says, "It all comes down to a lack of supervision. Broken bones, allergy attacks—"

"You're really going to blame me for this?" Mom slams her palms on the table. "What, so I'm beating up Jonah in between poisoning Jesse, that's it? I guess I'm making Will cry, too!"

I say, "Mom."

Dad says, "Damn it, Cara!"

Jesse appears from the living room, rubbing the red around his eyes. "What's going on in here?"

We all shut up.

He pads in, his socks making scuffle noises against the ground, pulls me up, and takes me out of the kitchen with him.

"What is it?" I say.

"Shh."

"You're supposed to be asleep."

He brings me to Will's room and says, "Something's wrong with him. Pick him up."

Will gasps in air and keeps screaming.

"It might just be colic," I say.

Jess wearily pushes me toward the crib. "Jonah, pick him up."

He stands by while I hold our brother and bounce him on my shoulder. Jesse recoils his hands into his sleeves, afraid to touch.

fourteen

I SNAP MY HELMET UNDER MY CHIN, FLINCHING, like always, at the thought of the skin catching in the buckle. "Camera ready?"

Naomi says, "Just so you know, we don't have to do this." She twirls the wire cutters in her left hand. They glint in the moonlight.

"Shut up."

She bristles. "You already broke the hand today. And I'd think you'd want to be at home with Jesse."

"It's the wrong hand. And Jesse's asleep."

Of course he's asleep. It's four o'clock in the freaking morning.

Naomi shrugs and hoists her camera onto her shoulder. "Hell, who am I to stop you?"

Nobody. Nobody's anyone to stop me. I swipe my cast under my nose. "Walk me through it."

"We've got to get inside, first, Evel Knievel." She leans against the polished SPRING MANOR COUNTRY CLUB sign and cleans the wire cutters on her jeans. "Plan is, I cut any locks, you crash like a true Olympian, and we see how fast we can get in and out."

I stretch my arms behind my head and let my ribs pull, making sure everything's loose. "You sure the pool's empty?"

"Trust me, Jonah, I've got the janitor's daughter knowledge. Everyone drains their pools over the winter."

"Thank God for your blue-collar background."

"I know, right?"

An owl croons nearby—they're common here, but the sound's enough to make me prick with the feeling we're being watched.

The *who* sounds almost accusatory.

I taste cement in my mouth and I have to close my eyes and swallow a few times before it will go away. It's just nerves. It's not like it means anything.

I need to do this one, and I know it in all of my

unbroken bones. I need to get stronger. I need to get stronger. This is the way. Face-planting into this empty pool will be my salvation. It has to be.

It's even darker when I open my eyes.

"Nom," I say.

She's hard at work, breaking through the lock on the gate. "Almost got it."

"It's cold as hell out here."

She's wearing a black coat belted around her invisible waist. "Gloves in my pocket. You can grab one for your good hand."

I reach into her pocket and pull on a glove. I'm so sweaty that my nose instantly fills with the smell of wet wool.

She purses her lips and breaks through the lock. "There." She fixes her baseball cap and shoves her hands under her armpits. "Off we go."

We trudge through the wet grass until we come to the biggest pool. It's deepest in the middle and shallow on the sides, like a gigantic bowl set into the ground. Naomi and I stand at the edge, staring in.

"Fourteen feet in the middle," she says.

I nod. It looks deeper without water.

She boots up her camera. "That'll be quite the smack."

"I know."

She looks at me. "You really want to do this?"

I chew the inside of my lip. I could go home and listen to the baby scream, listen to Jesse's cough rattle all the shit in his chest, listen to Mom and Dad trade accusations. Or I could pitch myself off the edge of an empty swimming pool.

It's not a hard choice. "I want to do this."

"Okay." Her camera rings. "Whenever you're ready, partner."

She fades into the black and I stand by the border of the pool, planting my feet and swinging my arms like a swimmer on a diving board. The wind spikes the hair on the back of my neck.

I don't even know what bones I'm trying to break.

I guess whatever happens, happens.

The hard part is actually jumping. There's this battle between the brain and the body—I never know if I'm really going to go until the last minute. My brain has to defeat my will to live, so, in a way, it really is an accident. Every crash is a biological accident, if not a physical one.

I always preferred biology to physics, anyway.

I try to go, but my knees lock. All right. I say, "Count me off, Nom, okay?"

She's somewhere to my right, where she can get a good angle. "Okay. On three?"

I nod. The helmet strap digs into my chin.

"One. Two."

I don't hear her say three because I'm already falling.

The air whooshes under my helmet, into my ears, and there it is—exhilaration.

I hit the bottom. The first pain is just the usual dull ache, the impact slap of my body against the concrete. I brace myself for the real pain—it'll be awful, but at least I'm used to it.

But, oh.

I'm not used to this.

My entire arm is ripping off, and I feel every tendon and every muscle and every bone and my side's on fire and my body is crushing my body and it's orange orange orange hurt and it's awful, it's worse than anything's ever been.

As soon as I get air I start screaming.

Her footsteps cascade down the side of the pool and there's her hand on the back of my neck. "Tell me what hurts."

"Get me up! Get me up get me up!"

"Jonah—"

I scuffle my legs on the pavement until I can move enough to aim my torso toward Naomi. I grab her stupid coat and hold her, digging my fingers into her sides. I huff air in and out of my nose so I don't throw up. The nausea comes, but the pain is not gone. I sound like a dog. "My arm—"

"Jonah, wiggle your toes!"

I wiggle them all around and kick my feet, and she lets her breath go. She cradles my head and says, "Breathe. Breathe."

I whinny. "This is awful."

"Shh."

"Make it stop."

"I will. Shhh."

The back of my head explodes, and I'm drowning drowning drowning in the empty pool. I bury my face in Naomi and scream, letting the pain take me away.

fifteen

JESSE FLIES INTO MY HOSPITAL CUBICLE, SWEAT ON his stubbly upper lip, hands in the air. "What the fuck?"

I throw my good hand over my face. "I told Naomi not to call you."

"Yeah, and I told *you* not to do this. Seriously, Jonah, what the hell? You didn't get enough ER fun today?"

I mumble, "Technically that was yesterday."

He had to drive almost an hour to get here. This is some grody community clinic just out of state—you've got to keep switching hospitals in this life.

He had to drive almost an hour to get here.

He paces back and forth, his hands in fists. "This has to stop. Jesus Christ, Jonah. This has got to stop."

"I know."

He leans against the yellow walls, staring at the ceiling like he's trying to think of a solution. The drip of the morphine into my IV is excruciating in its slowness.

Over the intercom, Nurse Glenda's called to the desk.

I say, "How you feeling?"

"I'm *fine*, brother, Jesus Christ, but I'm so fucking . . . God, I'm worried about you." He sits at the foot of the bed and shrugs off his jacket. "God. Naomi said you were sobbing."

I move my arm and sit up, pulling my knees to my chest so I have somewhere to put my shaky chin. "My shoulder's a fracture-dislocation. Those hurt more than just a break."

He reaches out and touches my sling. All my pain and suffering, and I don't even get a new cast. Just this awkward-ass sling. "And the elbow?"

"That's fractured."

"Anything else?"

"Three more ribs."

+ 1 shoulder + 1 elbow + 3 ribs. Total = 24.

He squints. "Haven't you already broken your elbow?"

"That was the other one."

He sighs and leans back, running a hair through his curls. "Mom and Dad are going to be furious."

"They don't have to know. I don't need a new cast. Just a sling. I'll just tell them the wrist was sore. They don't have to know, and Charlotte doesn't either, or Max and Antonia. Nobody."

"Jonah. Your arm will look funny."

"I can make it look okay. Look. I can take care of this," I insist. "I can make this okay."

He keeps messing up his hair. "How's the pain?"

I shake my head, staring at the quilt.

"Was it scary?"

The crash flashes through my mind like an awful Claymation film. I see my body melt into the pavement, into Naomi, see it filling the empty pool.

He lowers his voice—pitch, not volume. "Brother, you okay?"

The fourth feeling is worry.

I say, "Can you sit with me until Naomi comes back? Sh-she's getting ice chips."

"Uh-huh."

I scoot to the side of my bed and pat the mattress next to me. He sits beside me, fists on his knees, and doesn't cough. We don't touch, but the comfort bridges the gap between us.

No regrets.

sixteen

AT SCHOOL, CHARLOTTE SAYS, "SO JESSE'S OKAY now?"

"Yeah, he's in Statistics." I roll my pencil across the desk, trying to make the rigid turn of my broken elbow look casual. "It was a rough one for him, though. He's pissed off about it still."

"Yeah, you said." Charlotte pushes her hair behind her ears. "How'd Naomi take it?"

"Hmm?"

"You know how she is about Jesse. They've always been close."

"Well, she was concerned. We all get concerned. Jesse has a reaction, and it's like a fucking war's on. It's scary as hell. Mom's all jumpy and self-deprecating. You should have seen her washing his lunch this morning."

"My sister was worried."

The little bit of a smile I had sinks into my lips.

"What?" she says, plucking a petal off her carnation.

"I just don't think it's going to work. With Jesse and your sister."

"Did you ask him?"

"No."

"Then how do you know?" Her eyebrows bend together. "My sister's a sweetheart."

"I'm sure she is. I just don't think he's ready."

"He's sixteen."

"Yeah, and he's been out of the hospital for five minutes. Your sister eats peanut butter, gives my brother a kiss on the cheek, and me and my parents are ID'ing Jess's body."

She rolls her eyes. "If you want to baby someone, use Will. Jesse's a big boy."

"Yeah, a big, sick boy." I flip open my notebook.

She shakes her head. "You know, I worry about you. What's with the sling?"

"Wrist was just sore. Trying to get a break from gravity."

Mrs. Yanovic waddles in, four pens clasped between

her teeth. "Welcome to polyatomic ions, kids. Wait, McNab." She nods at me. "Miss Marlin wants you in her office."

I look at Charlotte and mumble, "Who's Miss Marlin?"

"Counselor."

"The counselor?"

She nods.

"It's probably a mistake." I gather my stuff. "She probably wants Jesse." Everyone always thinks it's their place to comfort him after a reaction. I don't even know.

Whatever. Anything to get out of Chemistry.

I tramp down the hall in my backpack, considering my options. My arm's throbbing, and I just want to go home, but I don't want to deal with Mom whining that she's not good enough, or that Dad doesn't appreciate her, and I can't stand listening to Will any longer. I want to go to the library and curl up and take a nap.

I want to go back and get Charlotte and do some kissing.

I take my cell phone out and text message Jesse. WHATS UP.

Just want to be sure, you know. It seems like the counselor would want to talk to me if he died.

He says, SHUT UP IM IN CLASS.

Okay. Good.

I eventually find Miss Marlin. Her door's squeezed between the principal's office and the supply closet. On an importance spectrum, she's much closer to the latter.

I knock with my cast.

"Come in."

Miss Marlin's a small black woman with paintbrush-thin fingers. Her sweater is pretty ugly.

"Hi."

She has a file in her lap. "Are you Jonah McNab?"

"Uh-huh."

She waves for me to sit down. The chair is too comfortable.

"How's everything going, Jonah?"

This question is enough to piss me off. I hate counselors. I hate how they pretend they're your best friend when they fucking don't know you. I got a counselor when Mom and Dad separated for the first time. I got a counselor when they got back together. I got one when they worried Jess was getting too much attention.

I have Naomi. I don't need this crap.

"I'm fine."

She nods. "Heard there was a scare with your brother yesterday."

"He's fine."

What a bitch. She doesn't know Jesse. How dare she sit there and look concerned.

She's got this white-noise machine, like she doesn't want the principal or the janitor to hear me if I start to cry. Yeah. I'm just on the verge of fuckin' tears, here.

"How's everything at home?"

I lean onto my elbows. My ribs don't like this. I ignore them. "Do you have a point?"

She nods once. "How'd you break your arm, Jonah?"

"Fell off my skateboard."

"And the black eye?"

"Fell off my skateboard."

"Your jaw?"

I stare at her. "You want me to say it again?"

"Jonah." She scoots forward in her chair and looks at me like she means it. I imagine her practicing this at night: scooting toward the side of her bed, making doe-eyes at the mirror.

She says, "This isn't the first time you've come in banged up. And this isn't the first time a couple of your teachers have come to me with concerns."

"There's nothing wrong with me. I'm just a klutz."

"I understand that you're seventeen, that you feel like you're old enough to take care of this yourself. And I hope you understand that I'm obligated to look for signs of abuse."

Abuse.

I think about what this word means.

I mean, obviously this chick thinks my parents hit me. And I know they never have.

But if I flinch every time they reach toward me, is that just as bad?

If my baby brother won't stop crying?

If I know, flat-out know, that they could take better care of Jesse, that they use him as an excuse to fight . . . you can't convince me that that's not just as bad.

"They don't hit me," I say. "I just take a lot of risks."

"Your brother—"

"My brother has a schizophrenic immune system. It has nothing to do with my parents. Check out his record. He makes enough school days. His grades are great. He's a good kid. None of this has anything to do with my parents."

"None of what, Jonah?"

Aw, shit. "None of my broken bones and none of Jesse's allergies. Look, I appreciate your concern, and if my parents ever beat the shit out of me, I'll be sure to come in. But I'm fine and so's Jesse. Your interference is not going to help."

And then . . . oh.

What if I break so many bones that I can't dodge

these accusations? What if they decide Mom and Dad are hitting me?

What if they decide they're not fit to be parents?

What happens to Will?

What happens to Jesse?

"Look," I say, desperate. "I'm rebellious. I'm attention-starved. My parents are busy with Jesse and the new baby. So I take risks and I get hurt. It's not their fault. They're good parents. Honestly. They call ambulances for Jesse. They watch whatever he eats. And they hold Will all the time. Dad sings him lullabies. They love them."

She leans even farther forward. She's about to fall out of her chair. "What about you?"

"They love me, too. Really, they do. None of this is their fault. Don't make them come in."

She says, "Well, we might need to—"

"No. If you need to discuss this more, just call me in here. Don't make them come in." I stand up. "I've got to go."

When I get outside her office, I'm so antsy I can't keep still. I text message Naomi, who doesn't need much coaxing to skip class. We sit on top of her car and smoke cigarettes.

I cough a little bit. I'm not an experienced smoker, but it's not my first cigarette either. I don't embarrass myself.

"So what are you breaking next?" she asks.

I say, "I think I'll stick with the cigarette for now," I say. "You know. Try normal teenage self-destructive."

She forces herself to laugh, and I force myself to keep smoking.

Don't think about the toes. Don't think about the cheekbone.

Just keep smoking.

seventeen

AT LUNCH, I FIND JESSE HIDING OUT IN THE WEIGHT room, squeezing his biceps together on a machine that looks like a torture device. His sneakers are dirty and untied.

"You wouldn't believe my morning."

He looks up. "Hey, brother."

"Hey." I flop down on the mats and lean against the radiator, squishing around my sling. The heat is heaven on my sore neck. "So the counselor thinks Mom and Dad are breaking my bones."

He raises his eyebrows. "Together? Like, one of them holds you down and the other one twists?"

"This is serious, Jess." I look around to make sure

we're safe to discuss this. The only other person in here is a runner on the treadmill all the way in the back. His iPod's on so loud that I'm surprised I can hear me and Jesse's conversation.

Jesse says, "I know it's serious," and adds twenty more pounds to the machine. "Look. You can't say nobody warned you. Of course they're going to suspect this."

"So what am I supposed to do?"

"Hmm." Jesse starts another rep. "One would suggest that you could stop breaking your bones."

"Shh."

"You want to be serious, Jonah? This needs to stop. I can't watch this."

"Stop it."

"You like watching me in the hospital, brother?"

"Don't ask me that."

"Yeah, well, I don't like seeing you like this, either." He frowns and counts under his breath. He's just pissed-off all over the place, this one. It's not unexpected—he's usually a bitch for a day or two after a reaction—but it's still a change from the Jess I know and love.

I say, "Hey. I brought you an apple."

He doesn't look up. "Did you wash it?"

"Of course."

"I'm not really hungry. So I talked to Naomi."

"Yeah?"

"She thinks you're on a mission."

"Oh."

"So, are you?" He drills me with those postanaphylactic bloodshot eyes.

"On a mission?"

"That's right, Captain."

I pull my knees up to my chest. "I don't think the kind of mission Naomi means."

"Look." He pauses, leans forward, pulls the bottom of his T-shirt like he's trying to make it bigger. "If you're trying to prove something—"

"Prove what?"

"That they're bad parents." He drops onto the ground beside me. "You know I wouldn't last a second in foster care."

"Jess, hush the hell up. That's not even a possibility."

"They could totally get convicted of something. You've got like eighty-five broken bones. How much more proof would a judge need?"

"Twenty-four."

Some scrawny sophomore walks by and considers the free weights. Jesse and I stare at him until he leaves and we can continue talking. The runner picks up his pace.

I watch him. "You wouldn't be in foster, anyway," I say.

He rubs his nose. "Yeah?"

"I'd take you. I'm the only one any court would trust to take care of you."

Jesse freezes, his teeth on his lip.

I say, "What?"

Jess says, "Shit, man. Let's do it."

"Jesse."

"Come on, I can't live in that house anymore. You know how Mom and Dad are." The timer on his cell phone goes off and he fishes two pills out of his pocket.

"They're annoying," I say. "That doesn't mean they're bad parents. Be honest."

"Okay, you want honest? I'm allergic to all that shit they feed the baby. I'm allergic to the liquid dripping out of Mom. I'm practically allergic to the damn house."

"I know. It sucks."

He swallows the pills. "So don't lie. You and I . . . we get along great. We'd be better without them."

I rub my hair. "Yeah, socially, maybe."

"So tell the counselor Mom and Dad are hitting you." God, his eyes are like red stars. "And, bam. It's just us."

"Okay, great. And I pay your medical bills . . . how, exactly?"

He curls up like I've punched him. "Fuck you."

But of course I can't quit. I offer the apple again. "And what about Will? They're not going to leave him with Mom and Dad if they think they're going to slap him around."

He makes that noise in his throat. "We could take Will."

"Jess, you can't even *touch* Will."

He shoves the apple out of my hand and it falls to the floor, rolls across the mats. "There. Can't eat it now."

"Jesse."

"Do you want to go?" he says.

I don't, but I leave anyway. I'm afraid to push him too far, at this point. At most points.

eighteen

I SWITCH TWO FOREIGN FILMS INTO ALPHABETICAL order. "So now he's basically entertaining the fantasy that we can get emancipated and live happily ever after. He actually wants this to happen. He's like the kid who wants to drop out of middle school."

Antonia takes the movies off the shelf and switches them back. "I'm sure you can get state money or something."

"Do you not know the alphabet?" I fix the movies. "He needs health insurance."

"*You* need health insurance," Max calls from the register. He starts ringing up this tall guy renting a shitload of bad porn. He gives the guy a look. "Want me to throw in *Sound of Music*, no charge? You'd have yourself a par-tay."

I cross my eyes and let the DVD covers blur together.

"Is your shoulder broken, Jonah?"

"That's not the point."

"They have government funding for these things," Antonia says.

"What about the baby?"

"I'm sure you have an aunt or something that would love him."

The man collects his movies and leaves. The bell on the door jingles, and Max sticks out his tongue and crosses his arms.

I say, "This is ridiculous. I can't believe we're even discussing this." And yet I keep going. "It's not about the money. I couldn't take care of Jess."

Antonia walks behind the counter and wraps her arms around Max. "You won't be all broken forever. You'll heal eventually."

"No. You don't get it. I can't take care of him. As in, I take crappy care of Jesse."

Max says, "Come on. I've seen you with him. You're a good brother."

I stand up—not to be dramatic, just to do something. I feel like moving. "He was covered in hives when I left him yesterday. He was already having the reaction. And I didn't do anything."

"You had no way of knowing."

"I let him get sick. All the time. I eat shit in front of him that he could get sick from breathing. I don't always wash my hands. I take terrible care of him."

Max straightens his glasses. "Didn't you save his life last year?"

I fold up on the floor. "Stop making me sound like a hero. The EpiPen's easy to do. You just jam the needle into his thigh. It doesn't make me an angel. It's a temporary fix, anyway. Just keeps him conscious long enough to get him to a hospital."

"It's significant, Jonah."

"Don't act like I can heal him. Seriously. Stop. I hate that." I wander over to the classics.

"He wants to live with you," Max calls. "That doesn't tell you anything?"

I ignore him and run my fingers over the spines of every happy-family-talking-dog DVD, swallowing the urge to explain the difference between a good brother and a loved one.

Then I hear Weezer through the front door and, in spite of everything, I'm smiling. "That's my ride."

"All right, get out of here." Max shakes his head, like there's something more he wanted to say.

"What?"

"Nothing. Go have fun with your girlfriend."

People keep telling me where to go.

"She's not my girlfriend."

Charlotte dances in her car, her hair whipping back and forth. I climb into the passenger seat and buckle in. "Hello."

"Hey."

She takes off out of the parking lot, the turbocharge on the Jetta growling from good use. The CD player clicks into a new song.

"So what are we doing tonight?" she asks.

I settle into the seat. "I don't care. Let's just stay out forever."

She laughs. "And what are we supposed to do to keep us entertained forever?"

"I don't need to be entertained. I just need this."

Out of nowhere, her eyes go all serious. She touches my cast. "How are you doing this?

"Doing what? My hand? I hit a wall by accident."

"By *accident*?"

"Don't worry."

She's quiet for a minute while we join the bigger roads. I swallow and concentrate on the music, the constant *woosh* of street noise.

I stare at the window. "Man. You know, someday we're gonna be stronger, Charlotte."

"Oh, yeah?"

"Yeah. Someday we'll be beyond this."

I don't know who I'm including in "we." Or I do know, but I'd rather not think about it. I'd rather just let it hang in the air and pretend that will make it true.

"Yeah," she says. "I'll be a singer, you'll be an architect. We'll live happily ever after."

This scenario hardly answers all my questions, but it's enough for now.

We decide on this diner with crappy food and four tables. We share French fries and ketchup and start talking about each other.

Our words rain down in a hurricane. We could do this forever.

I guess I haven't made it clear how I feel about Charlotte. Well, she puts my heart in a microwave and watches as it warms up and explodes. When I'm around her, my blood runs hot and thick. It's beautiful.

You could say there's nothing special about her. You could make the case.

But, really, she's special because nobody else can do the microwave thing.

"Do you have to babysit on Halloween?" she asks.

My parents go to this Halloween event every year.

High-school partying for religious grown-ups. "No. Jess'll be at home."

"There's a party at Marten's," she says. "You want to go?"

I drag a French fry through some mustard. "I sort of hate Halloween."

She frowns. "If this is you trying to get out of going somewhere with me—"

"No. This is me sort of hating Halloween."

She nods, chewing on her lip. "Then let's go to a water park, all right?" She's got ketchup on her lips, like blood. I want to kiss it off and fix it and make it better. "When it gets warm."

"What about tonight?"

"Sleigh ride?"

"It's October," I say.

"Hay ride?"

I shake my head. She sips her soda.

I suggest, "Roll in the hay?"

"Jonah."

"Damn. Well, you can't blame a guy for trying."

She sets down her glass. "We're not even dating."

"So we can't have sex?"

She rolls her eyes, her tongue poking out the side of her mouth.

"It's an honest question."

"It's a stupid one. You know how I feel."

I don't know why I have to honor her feelings when she isn't honoring mine. But whatever. I'm not an asshole.

She plays with her carnation. It's pink and starting to brown along the edges. Pans rattle back in the kitchen, and I spend a moment just looking at this beautiful girl.

I could stay here forever. I look at her easy smile and I know that I'm already enough for her. That I don't need stronger bones or a stronger heart for this to be okay.

She reaches out and takes my hand. I nod to myself, staring at the French fries.

Enough screwing around, Jonah. It's time to face facts. This breaking thing . . . it's time to stop. This is when I decide.

nineteen

THE TROUBLE COMES WHEN IT'S TIME TO GIVE this news to Naomi. She bounds up to me on Monday before third period, a handful of Web printouts in her fist, and then she's showing me pictures of people bleeding and people in traction and people's bones oozing infection. "We're going to have to be very careful with the next one," she whispers, shoving the pages into my locker.

"Look," I say, and I know I should be breaking the news to her, but instead I dive into my pocket and come up with my physics test. "Look at this."

She sees the A and her face breaks into a smile. "Jonah! That's awesome!"

"It's not just awesome, babe." I rip a piece of a Post-it note and stick the test to the inside of my locker. "It's another deposit on a ticket out of here. Architect school—"

"You want to celebrate?" And she makes a breaking motion with her hands.

Oh, Naomi. She does this all the time. She gets way too wrapped up in what she's doing. It's like her thing.

One time we did this report on the 1960s, and she tie-dyed her carpet and stopped eating meat.

One time we learned about the Atlantic Ocean and she filled her entire bedroom with fish tanks.

Now she looks up at me, her pointed chin tilted to the side. Her eyes are huge and humid.

"I don't think I'm going to do this anymore."

"We can do something about the pain," she says immediately. "I've been looking into it. If you take a lot of cough medicine before—"

"Naomi, stop. It's not about the pain. I can't do this anymore."

Her mouth bends toward the ground. "But why not?"

I love that Naomi needs a reason for me to stop killing myself. What a friend.

"It's not fair," I say. She's big on fairness. "I'm ripping my family to shreds. That wasn't the point."

"I know it wasn't."

"This is too much for my parents right now. They've got to focus on Jesse."

"Jonah, come on." She takes my good arm and pulls me to the hallway window seat. With the sun howling beside us and the hordes of people rushing by, I feel like I'm sitting by a river.

"Look, kid," she says. "You can't stop now."

I shake my head. "You're insane."

"No, listen. I know this is getting hard." She traces her fingers down my cast. "You're brave as hell, you know that?"

"Don't do this."

"No. I don't want you to think I don't appreciate this." A cloud moves in front of the window, and Naomi's face gets dark. "What you're doing is . . . shit, it's a fucking revolution."

"Nom."

"Look, I'm proud of you! You're telling everyone that this is your body and what you do with it is your business. That takes balls, man."

"That's not what I'm doing."

"You're brave."

"I'm *desperate*." God, people really needed to stop making me sound like some kind of hero.

"Naomi," I say. "If people think my parents are hitting me, they'll take Will and Jesse away from them. Will is fucking eight months old. He needs his parents. And how the hell is Jesse supposed to survive on his own?" I cut her off before she can start. "Stop. This isn't okay. I never should have started this, and you know it."

She swallows and I see all the muscles in her throat. "So we'll be more careful," she says. "We can just do fingers and toes and stuff."

"Nom, what the hell? What do you get from this?"

"The video—"

"Don't lie. It's not the video."

She smiles and stares down at the window seat. "I don't want to tell you. It's stupid."

I realize the sun's back.

"Tell me anyway."

She plays with the upholstery. "You're going for it, man." She shrugs. "You're putting your all into something. It's . . . um, kind of inspiring?"

"It's self-torture. Not exactly inspiring. Or even interesting."

"It's not self-torture. Don't belittle it like that." She shakes her head. "Don't pretend that's why you're doing it. Just because it will make it easier to stop."

I don't say anything.

"You want to get stronger. You want to be a better person."

"Jesus Christ, Naomi, I'm not some sort of martyr. I'm not even a novelty. *Everyone* wants to be a better person."

"But you're going for it." She throws her arms around my neck. It's like hugging a doll. "I love you."

"Yeah, yeah."

"So don't stop," she whispers. "Keep inspiring me."

All best friends are the same because you'll do anything for them.

She'd do it instead, if I asked. She'd break her neck for me.

"I'll think about," I say.

Aw, shit.

twenty

NEXT DAY DURING DINNER, NO JESSE. INSTEAD,
just the *squeak squeak squeak* of his arms on the rowing
machine.

And Will shrieks.

Dad leads grace then slices into his chicken breast.
"Did Jesse eat already?"

"He's not eating," I say, and stick a piece of cheese in
Will's mouth. He spits it out.

Squeak squeak squeak.

"What do you mean, he's not eating?"

"He means he had a smoothie," Mom says, reaching
for a drumstick.

Will bangs his hands in his strained carrots.

I say, "No. I mean he's not eating. He hasn't eaten all day. I don't think he's eaten since the hospital."

"Of course he has."

"I really don't think so."

Because I keep offering him food and he keeps blowing me off. Because the blender's sparkly clean. Because he's pale as hell.

Dad looks at me. "Why are you wearing that sling?"

"My wrist is sore. Can we talk about Jesse?"

He cuts into his meat. Only my father would use a knife and fork to eat fried chicken. He's still in his suit. "If he weren't eating, he'd be having trouble."

"No, he wouldn't. He'd probably be healthier. I think that's the point. The only way he could have an attack would be by, you know, touching Will's shit you leave lying around."

"Language, Jonah!"

"Stuff."

I hear them both exhale.

"So, what's the problem?" Mom says. "He's afraid of having another reaction?"

She says it like it's an irrational fear. Sometimes I really don't think she gets how terrifying the reactions are.

"I can't read his mind, Mom. I just know he's not

eating. Maybe because he can barely breathe in this house as it is—"

"Don't exaggerate."

I hear them both keep breathing.

Squeak squeak squeak.

Baby screaming.

I take a thigh from the fried chicken bucket.

"Just give him some time," Dad says.

"How long? An hour? A week?"

Dad straightens his tie. "Come on. He'll be fine."

End of discussion. Apparently we're fine!

Mom and Dad have Bible study and Jesse blows out to some kind of sports practice, so I stay home with the baby. I lie on my bed with my eyes closed, while he crawls along my carpet and cries intermittently. I try very hard not to think. About why the damn baby won't stop crying. About how skinny Jess can get.

My hand twitches toward the hammer beside me.

Why do I have a hammer?

Because I took it from downstairs.

For Naomi. For me. I exhale.

This isn't how it's supposed to work, Jonah.

If you have a problem with Jesse, deal with Jesse.

Don't take it out on your toes.

I look at them and wiggle the eight I didn't break in

the first skateboard crash. Might as well walk while I can, I decide, and head downstairs.

Because I just don't want to think about Jesse right now.

I plop Will in his high chair and open the refrigerator. Just the thought of eating half this crap makes me want to throw up. My jaw's killing me, so I settle on a milkshake. I'll make up for the calories Jess isn't getting.

I scoop chocolate ice cream and milk into the blender, and it takes me like an hour to find the button to make it spin. No one uses this blender but Jesse. I pour my milkshake into a glass and end up with half of it on the floor. And of course we're out of paper towels. "Stay in the chair," I tell Will, and he looks like he nods through his tears. It's the first flash of sweetness I've ever gotten from the kid, and I scoop some milkshake into his mouth as a reward. He actually smiles.

He babbles while I tilt some milkshake into a sippy cup for him. He spills all over the tray of his high chair and starts crying again.

All good things end, I guess.

He splashes in the brown puddle. He's got milkshake all over him. I tweak him on the nose and venture into the garage for a new roll of paper towels.

I hear footsteps in the kitchen—definitely not Will—

and when I return, Jess stands by the table, stripping off his layers of hockey clothes.

I say, "What are you doing home?"

"Practice was canceled."

I turn away from him to hang the paper towels up. His gloves and coat rustle as he pulls them off.

He says, "What the hell has Will got on him?"

"Don't touch—"

I turn around and there's Jesse, his hand on Will's sticky arm.

"Jesse, shit, I told you don't touch him!" I grab Jesse's arm and yank him away. There's milkshake on his hand. Oh shit, shit, shit.

Will takes his yelling up a hundred decibels.

I force Jess to the sink and hold his hand under the water. His whole hand is swollen. God. He's so bad with milk. This is so bad. This is so bad.

And I could take care of him so much fucking better if I had two hands.

"What is it?" he says. His voice is that forced calm.

"Chocolate milkshake."

"The hives, man."

They're up to his shoulder already. His arm is almost twice the size of the other.

"Ow," he breathes.

"Shit. Shit. Shit." And he's even standing in the puddle I spilled. This is unbelievable. I can't . . . how the hell did I do this?

I'm *such* an idiot.

"What the hell were you doing?" he says. "Why didn't you clean him up?"

"I didn't think you were home—"

"Why the hell were you using my blender, anyway?"

God. I take the only clean thing he has in the whole house, and I put milk and chocolate in it.

I should be shot.

Washing isn't working. His face is swelling. He's got hives all over his neck and if they're in his neck, they're about to be in his throat.

"Sit down." I push him into the living room and yell to him while I root through the cabinets. "Don't scratch!"

"What the fuck kind of harm is that going to do now?" He shudders and breathes, and I hear every muscle in his throat. I hear the deep, deep whistle in his chest.

My hand freezes on the bottle of Benadryl. "Can you breathe?"

He doesn't answer, and that's all I need.

When your little brother's about to die, for a second it doesn't matter that it's your fault and you're scared to death and you only have one arm. For a second, you turn into a robot.

I snatch the bottle from the shelf and wrench off the cap. I stand over him with one foot on his knee and say, "Open your mouth."

I pour the pink syrup down his throat. Some leaks through the blue oxygen-starved skin of his lips and dribbles onto his chin. I cover his mouth with my hand. "You will not choke," I tell him. "You will not throw up. You will drink. You will get this all down."

He keeps trying to look into my eyes and I keep looking away. He's crying, but it's just fear, and it's just the immune response. It's not real. We're robots.

He swallows and I take my hand away.

"Breathe," I say. "Now."

He's coughing. His chest makes noises like a truck.

I'm clutching the EpiPen.

In his high chair, Will positively howls.

"Come on, man," I say.

And Jesse breathes.

When your little brother looks at you and you almost just destroyed him, you can't be a robot anymore.

He slumps onto me, more out of exhaustion than affection. His face is so red and hot. I lower the sticky bottle to the table. The guilt is a big ball of yarn at the bottom of my stomach. Breaking bones hurts less than this.

"You're okay," I say, and push him away because I might still have milk on me. "But look, man, we've got to get to a hospital."

He shakes his head. "I don't want to. I'm okay."

"Jesse."

He inhales—it's harsh, but it's there. "If the reaction spikes again, we'll go. But I'll just . . . I'll load up on Benadryl and I'll sleep it off."

"Man—"

"Come on, brother." He nails me with those teary eyes. "We were just at the hospital."

I stand up and walk away from him, toward the high chair. I've got to give Will a bath. "You're being ridiculous. I am not going to let you—"

"What will Mom and Dad say?"

I'm quiet.

"If they find out I'm having a reaction because of something you did, they won't listen to you anymore. They'll stop taking you seriously when you tell them to clean up. They'll use it against you all the time."

I close my eyes and lean over the high chair. "Hush, Jesse."

"They will never trust you to take care of me. Come on, Jonah."

"Stop."

"Come on. Don't do it. Don't call an ambulance. I hate ambulances."

He really does. He always says I could get him there faster.

Not that I could drive him right now. I'm so fucking useless.

"Don't make me go, Jonah."

Will screams, and I turn away from him and face Jesse, and I put my hands in my hair. "All right!" I say. "All right. Stay here."

Jesse stares at his lap, quietly triumphant.

"Stay here," I say.

I send Jesse up to his room—he'll bang on the floor if he needs me—and I clean everything and give Will a good bath in the sink. I scrub him so hard I can't even blame him for screaming. But I do anyway.

It's a horrible, metallic relief to be away from Jesse. I pick up the phone.

And ten minutes later the doorbell rings and there she is. She stands on my doorstep with a handful of tulips. One red blossom peeks out of her bun.

I say, "Charlotte."

"I'm right here. Are you all right?"

I want to hold her, but I've got the baby. She reaches

out and takes him, and the freedom to not be responsible for him anymore is almost as good as a hug.

She shakes the flowers. "Can I bring these or are flowers not good?"

My throat is stuck or I'd say that say flowers are fine, but since I can't she leaves them in our garden. I stop her before she unpins the one in her hair.

"Where is he?" she says. "Upstairs?"

"Uh-huh. I just checked him. He's fine. I made him take more Benadryl—"

She kisses both my cheeks and pulls me down next to her on the couch. "Just calm down, honey."

"I . . . God, I can't believe you're here."

"Of course I'm here. You called."

"This was all my fault."

She says, "I'm sure it wasn't."

"No. It was. I was making a milkshake and I gave some to Will and Will was a mess, and I just left him there. I just left him there for Jess to touch."

"Jonah, calm down."

"I messed everything up." I wish I could cuss in front of Charlotte because I could seriously use a scream right now.

She holds me, my head against her chest. My face is right next to Will's.

I make sobbing *huh-huh-huh* noises to match his cries.

"Jonah, shhhh." She strokes my hair. "Shh. He's okay now."

"It'll happen again."

"Shhh."

"It's gonna happen again."

"Oh, sweetheart . . ."

There's nothing for her to say, but it helps to have my head on her boobs.

I'm hysterical, not unconscious.

"This is not your fault," she says. "It's just something that happened. So just take some deep breaths, and tell me if I can do anything to help."

"Just don't leave me here alone with Jess and the baby. Just stay, okay?"

"Okay."

Charlotte makes me tea, and I kiss her.

She imitates her choir director and jokes about her Biology grades, and she laughs, and I laugh, and I don't know if it's inappropriate to be happy right now, but she holds me so close and I feel her and I touch her.

Charlotte is a prism for my life. Without her, my existence looks pale and bleak and somewhere near the middle of the suck-meter. But around her, I see clearly that my life isn't made up of anything mediocre, but instead is some combination of the amazing and the dreadful— my brother who adores me, my parents who want what's best for me, my brother who's dying, my parents who won't understand me. It's not gray at all; it's too painfully colorful and fantastic and awful for me to see without her help.

And sometimes I realize all that color is too much.

"Someday it will be better," I tell her.

She kisses me. "I know."

"I can't wait."

She can, and that's the main difference between us.

We watch game shows and feed the baby and tuck him in and listen to him cry over the baby monitor. I check on Jesse every hour or so, and he wakes up and starts his homework. Charlotte doesn't tell me she loves me, but she lets me put my head in her lap, and for the few hours she's with me, I'm happy. Really.

But she leaves at ten, an hour before Mom and Dad come home. "Where's Will?" Mom says, setting her dog-eared paperback on the counter. Dad undoes her necklace—I'll never understand why they dress up for book club.

"I put him to bed."

"Jesse?"

"He's in his room." And my mouth is cottony with worry and I say, "He had a reaction. I think he's all right now."

Dad loosens his tie. "How bad?"

"It was pretty bad. He took a lot of Benadryl. But he's feeling a lot better. And he looks okay."

"What happened?"

And I know Jesse's right. I know that if I tell them the truth, I'm risking their trust forever. I'm risking the unhealthy bond they've allowed me to have with Jesse.

"It was my fault," I say, my head down. "I had a milk-shake and I didn't clean up."

I can leave Will out of it, at least.

Mom crosses her arms, "Jonah—"

"I know." I cover my eyes. "I know I know I know I know I know."

"You've just got to be more—"

I can't take this lecture, not now. My stomach is crawling and I can't take it I can't take it I can't take it.

"I've got to talk about this later," I say. "I just can't do this right now."

I start up the stairs. Mom starts to call me but Dad says, "Let him go," like he's some sort of parenting expert.

I sit on my floor with my ear against Jesse's wall, trying to listen to his breathing around Will's cries.

That hammer is still here. I pick it up and hold the cold head in my palm. My mind is an explosion of Naomi and Jesse and Charlotte and Mom and Dad and Miss Marlin and I can't *do* this right now, and I don't know what I want but I know it's definitely not this.

Will's voice gets higher and higher. Soon, only dogs will hear him and our ears will get a break.

Jesse coughs and my heart jumps with electricity.

I take off my shoe and, through my sock, smash each toe individually.

It doesn't hurt as badly as you might think. Each toe takes only one or two smacks to really snap.

I try to time my hammering so it matches Jesse's gasping. Every time I hear his breath snag, I swing the hammer.

Eight toes are broken in no time.

2 femurs + 1 elbow + 1 collarbone + 1 foot + 4 fingers + 1 ankle + 2 toes + 1 kneecap + 1 fibula + 1 wrist + 2 ribs + 1 jaw + 1 hand + 1 shoulder + 1 elbow + 3 ribs + 8 toes = 32 total.

174 to go.

I fall asleep in some painful, drunken state, Will's screams and Jesse's coughing lulling me into submission.

twenty-one

THE NEXT MORNING, MY FEET ARE SHARDS OF glass in a sock. I listen to Jesse on the rowing machine and Will sputtering in his crib until the dizziness tapers enough for me to crawl to my computer.

I Google "broken toes."

I Google "food allergies."

I Google "I'm so dizzy I can't see straight."

I Google "child abuse."

I Google "Am I going to die?"

None of the answers are helpful, although the last one takes me to some creepy links that at least distract me for a minute.

The windows flash on the screen, and Jesse's rowing gets

faster and faster. I click on my Favorites folder and bring up one of my beloved Confucianism websites. When that Chinese music starts, I lie down on my floor and close my eyes. Begging to sink in, zone out, ignore the baby.

He shouts something, his eight-month-old version of speech, and I wrinkle my nose.

Shut up shut up shut up everyone just shut up.

Mom yells, "Damn it, Will, stop crying!"

That's it. I need to do something about these toes. "Jesse!" I bang my cast against the floor. "Jess, come up here!"

The rowing stops. I picture him listening, straining his ears over the baby.

"Jess, come here!"

I picture him considering.

My door opens and there's Mom, her tawdry pink robe washing her whole face gray, Will propped on her shoulder. "Need something, hon? Why are you on the floor?"

I raise my head. Mom spins. "Just need to talk to Jesse."

She crosses her arms. "Do you need to talk about last night?"

"I screwed up."

"I know it was just an accident. And you're so good with him."

But . . .

She says, "But you just need to be more careful, Jonah. How are the injuries?"

My voice feels glued somewhere near the crown of my head. When I talk, I sound more like Dad or Jesse than myself. "I'm fine."

Will starts screaming again, and she says something I can't hear.

I end up sleeping through the time it takes Mom and Will to leave and Jesse to arrive. He wakes me up with one hand on my chest. "You look like crap."

"I think I'm sick."

"I think you're in pain."

"Oh. Yeah."

"So what'd you do?"

I point toward my feet. "They need to be taped up. I am so nauseous."

"Okay. Hold on." He handles my feet, and I grit my teeth. He starts talking, probably just to distract me. "I did five reps," he says. "And an hour of rowing. I'm really building up my stamina. I think it's going to make a difference for hockey. You're coming to my game tonight, right?"

I try not to moan. "Of course."

"So . . . what are you doing for Halloween?"

When I was little, I always got mad at Jesse because he wouldn't come trick-or-treating with me. I don't know how it took me so long to figure out that it would kill him, but ever since, Halloween gives me a sour sort of taste.

I say, "Will I be able to walk?"

He inhales as the socks come off. "Shit. Yeah, don't worry. We can work this out. Hold on."

He rushes to the bathroom and I get my first good look at what I've done. My toes look like raw chicken nuggets sewn into my foot. They're purple and stick in incorrect directions. One of my nails is falling off.

Jesse returns with a shitload of gauze and medical tape, as if we really have the supplies to fix all of this.

"When did you do it?" he asks, ripping a piece of tape with his teeth.

"Last night. I wasn't exactly thinking straight."

He starts taping the toes together. I dig my fingers into the floor. He says, "I don't think you've ruined anything, here."

This is a funny way of putting it.

"They should heal okay."

"I know.

"I'm worried about you. This is beginning to look more and more like one of those suicide cry-for-attention things."

I start hitting my head against the ground. "You're not supposed to just ask me that. You're supposed to dance around the subject and call a hotline if you're so fucking concerned."

He lowers his voice. "Jonah, what's up?"

"Nothing." I flap my arms over my face. He tapes me and it hurts. "What's up with you?" I snap. "Why aren't you eating?"

"I am eating." Rip of more tape. "This one might hurt."

I chew my tongue. "Is this like an eating disorder?"

"I'm allergic to everything. It's already like the ultimate eating disorder."

I throw my hands away. "Look, if you don't eat, you're going to get worse. You're going to lose tolerance and you won't be able to eat *anything*. If you think starving's fun now, wait until you don't have any choice."

"I'm eating."

"Stop blowing me off."

He pulls one of my toes and I swear. "I am not blowing you off," he says, "but you have some nerve to lecture me about how to take care of myself. Now shut up and let me finish here."

I exhale. "We're gonna be really late."

"It's okay. I'll drive fast."

I say, "I don't know what to do with you."

"You've done enough." And it doesn't sound like a compliment.

"What?"

"Jonah, relax, okay? Just let me tape."

I could throw up.

He finishes, and I examine his handiwork. My toes are secured in a wonky line like drunk soldiers.

"All right. Here we go." Jess takes my good arm and hauls me off the ground. "You all right?"

My head's about to split open, but my feet feel okay. "Yeah."

"Just keep your weight on your heels and the tape should hold up."

"Thanks, brother."

"Uh-huh." He pulls his sweaty hair back in his fist. "I'm gonna shower. Get yourself a granola bar or something and let's get out of here."

"Okay."

He starts to go, then pauses with his hand on the door frame. "Jo."

"Problem?"

He shrugs. "Can you try to do something about the baby before we go?"

There's this desperation in his voice.

"I'll try," I say.

twenty-two

NAOMI'S WEARING MY SWEATSHIRT AGAIN, AND the cuffs are folded over but still cover her hands. She grumbles in the back of her throat. "I can't believe you did this without me."

"It was impulsive. Barely intentional."

"You couldn't have waited?"

I wiggle my shoulders. "No, I couldn't."

"You're like an addict."

"Hush. This isn't about you. Look, I have to stop doing this. For real. It's bothering Jesse."

"What's up with Jesse?"

"I don't even know." I lead her down the south hall-way. "Ever since his reaction he's been all weird and combative. He never used to argue with me, and now it's like . . . I don't know." My eyes feel like they're coated in sandpaper.

She crosses her arms. "I'll talk to him."

"He's not your responsibility." We arrive outside the AP Bio classroom just as the kids start pouring out. I watch them, one by one, each of them an Ivy League–bound robot. Except my girl.

"He listens to me," Naomi says. "What the hell are we doing here, anyway?"

Charlotte emerges, her hair pinned up in a Spanish orchid.

My girl who knows real life like it's one of her songs.

Naomi fixes her baseball cap. "Oh."

I do my best to wrap up our conversation before Charlotte gets to me. "Just leave Jess alone. He's got enough on his plate. Figuratively."

"Fuck you."

I leave her to be pissed off and go bear-hug Charlotte. She giggles inside my arms, like a chorus of tiny violins.

"You smell fantastic," she says.

"Hey, backatcha."

I hear the smattering of combat boots and unbury my face from Charlotte's curls. Naomi is stomping away, making as much noise as she can.

Charlotte's lips peek open in her *what-the-heck?* face. "What's wrong with her?"

"No clue. She's mad about something."

"You know what it is, don't you?" She takes my arm and we stroll back toward our lockers. It's almost like she's my girlfriend. My feet hurt, but not so much that I care. "She's jealous."

"Please. Naomi would fall in love with you before she'd fall in love with me."

Charlotte says, "Hmm."

"She's not gay."

"Someone has to be gay."

"Well, not Naomi."

"Someone has to be." She takes a step back. "Are you limping?"

Shit.

"Jonah?"

I start walking ahead, this time without Charlotte on my arm. "I'm fine."

She follows. "Is your . . . is your *foot* broken?"

I take her hand. "Toes."

"Jonah! What's *happening* to you?" She plants her high heels on the linoleum and digs her fingers into my wrist until I have to stop. The hallway flow continues around us. We're an island, together.

And there's nothing for me to say.

"Skateboarding." I swallow. "You know how I am."

"No. You can't skateboard with three broken ribs."

I don't correct her with *Five*.

We face off. She's got this glitter on top of her eyes and she's so beautiful and so angry.

"Jonah," she whispers. "Tell me."

I close my eyes and pray for a trapdoor.

"Jonah."

I pray for a closed-over throat and no more breathing.

"Is it your parents?"

"No. It's not my parents."

My headache is back and it's destroying down to my neck and shoulders. I don't know if this is a sign of my trapdoor or my impending doom.

"Look," I say. "There isn't an answer for this that you're going to like."

She croaks, "Jesse?"

"Jesse would never hurt me. Seriously, Charlotte, let it go."

A speck of glitter flickers into her eye.

I see her thought process.

I see her crossing out every other possible option.

I see her chin shake.

She says, "Are you doing this yourself?"

I'm afraid I'm going to vomit on her pretty shoes. "Charlotte, I'm really not feeling well. Can we talk about this later?"

"No!"

But I'm not faking it, and I'm trembling so hard I almost fall over. She catches me, and I stabilize myself on a locker.

"Geez, are you sick?" she says.

"No, just . . . I can't talk about this right now." The bell rings. "Look, are you coming to Jesse's game tonight?"

She pauses, tongue against her cheek, and nods.

"Okay. We'll talk there, okay? You know where I'll be."

I don't know why I think this will help. Maybe I'm just stalling the inevitable. She knows. My only option is to confess and deal with the consequences.

But confessing to Charlotte will take a fuckload of courage. Of strength.

In short, I want to watch Jesse when I do it.

twenty-three

THE UNOFFICIAL FAMILY SPOT IS JUST BEHIND THE box. We'd have a great view of Jesse, if he were ever on the bench.

We used to all come together, but now Mom stays home with the baby. We never let the baby out of the house. I guess we're afraid what people will say if they see him crying like that.

I tap Dad on the shoulder. "Look at him."

He stops cheering and turns to me. "He's doing great."

"He's so *pale*."

Dad folds the sleeves on his sports jacket. "He's fine."

"He looks *sick*."

"Don't go that far."

"I'm going that far."

The puck heads straight to Jesse's stick, and we scream at him for a minute as he flies down the ice.

"His skating's off," I say.

"It's not."

"He's wobbly."

"Jonah. It's fine."

Dad's never going to get it. I don't care how many allergic sisters he had. She wasn't Jesse, and she didn't have his willpower. Nobody does.

I tear my eyes away from Jesse to scan the bleachers. "Do you see Charlotte?"

"Nope. No Naomi, either."

Right when he says this, though, I see Naomi standing on her backpack, leaning over the plastic shield that separates the bleachers from the ice. She pounds her mittened hands together and screams, "Come on, Jesse!" Her cheeks are blown fuchsia from the cold.

She really is cute for such a psycho.

The other team calls a time-out and Jess leans with his fists on his knees. His back's to us, and I can see how hard he's breathing. His shoulders fall and rise under his jersey.

I nudge Dad. "Look."

"Jonah, stop trying to scare me."

"He shouldn't be playing." I stand up and yell, "Jesse!" until he looks at me. I hold up both my thumbs, and he does it right back.

"See," Dad says. "He's all right."

Jess winks at Naomi and goes back to his heavy breathing.

"He's having trouble."

"Have faith. He will be okay."

My parents tend to turn to "Have faith" when they have no better defense. The thing is, they rarely seem to try faith themselves. They just expect me to do it for them. Maybe that's why they had children.

I yell, "Catch your breath, Jesse!"

He grumbles something back. He's too far away for me to hear, but my brother lip-reading sense tells me it's "I'm working on it."

"Get him out of there," I tell Dad, sitting down as the referee's whistle signals the end of time-out. "Talk to his coach or something."

"Jonah—"

I shut him up because there's someone heading toward us. And instead of Charlotte, it's a huge guy in a glen plaid suit.

Principal Mockler.

"Crap." I sit up straight. "Act normal."

Dad says, "What?"

"Principal's coming. Might want to pretend you're not letting your son die out there."

Mockler wades through the bleachers and looms over us. "Hello, there, Jonah. Mr. McNab."

Dad shakes hands and makes nice.

Mockler sits next to me. "Could I have a word with you, Jonah?"

I nod toward Jess. "I'm watching my brother."

"Jonah, there's something I'd like to discuss with you."

As if he can't tell I'm busy. As if he can't tell I'm obsessing over Jess right now.

"One of your friends came to talk to me," Mockler says. "She was concerned about your recent . . . appearance. Is everything all right at home?"

Dad looks over. He says, "If you're about to accuse me of something, you'd best wait until we're in a more professional setting."

Mockler straightens his tie and looks straight at me. "Maybe we should discuss this in private."

"They're not hitting me," I say, tracking Jess with my eyes.

"I'm more concerned you're doing this to yourself." Mockler says. "Jonah, listen. We have pretty clear—"

Before I can shut him up, Jesse falls to his knees.

I leap off the bleachers. "Get up, brother!" I shout.

Dad doesn't move, but Naomi's going crazy too. She hops up and down on her backpack, screaming, "Up, Jess! Get up!"

One of Jesse's teammates skates over and hauls him up, and I see them talking—teammate with his glove on Jesse's shoulder, trying to find out if Jess is okay. . . .

"Did Charlotte tell you?" I ask.

After a pause, he nods. I could probably get him fired for admitting that.

I point. "Look at my brother. Look at him."

"Jonah—"

I hear my voice rising—in pitch—as my head falls to pieces. "If you don't want your students hurting themselves, look at him. Look at my brother. He's not eating." I turn to my dad. "He's not eating!"

Dad stares like he doesn't even recognize me.

Like he never suspected I'd lose my mind over Jesse.

Naomi faces us, her hands on her face. She's bundled in her mittens and coat and scarf and I'm so, so overheated from just looking at her.

"We're going to need you to get a psychiatric evaluation,"

Mockler says, in a voice he must think sounds concerned. "We need to figure out why you're hurting yourself."

From the expression on my dad's face, you'd think he'd never had a self-destructive son before.

"Look at him!" I shriek.

On the ice, Jesse falls again. He gags onto the ice, and spit drips from his lip. I imagine it steaming.

"Look at my brother!"

Dad traps me under his arms and squeezes me. My ribs burn and he keeps squeezing and squeezing, until I have to stop shouting. Until I can't watch Jesse anymore.

twenty-four

SINCE BREAKING BONES DIDN'T WORK, I'LL TRY this new defense mechanism: disappearance.

I rip out of the hockey rink too quickly for anyone to see me. I'm a blur. Screw the toes—I'm lightning. I'm fucking gone, is what I am.

I'm in the parking lot before anyone catches me.

"Jonah!" Naomi skids beside me, tottering on her tiny legs. "What the hell was going on in there?"

I'm so fucking hot, despite the evening air. I tear off my jacket and force it at her. She takes it. My sling sways in the wind and my shoulder creaks back and forth.

"They think I'm crazy," I say. "Everyone thinks I'm crazy."

"Slow down."

Moonlight glints off the car tops. It's fucking seven o'clock; why is it so dark? I hate the fall.

"People are going to see your shoulder," she points out.

"I don't care. Can you get me out of here?"

Naomi—my partner in crime. My escape vehicle.

She licks her lips. "All right, fine. But I wanted to see Jesse."

I storm toward her car. "He's killing himself."

"His team will look after him."

"Nobody fucking knows how to look after him. That's the goddamn problem." I yank the passenger side door and collapse in the seat. My anger puffs my chest up and down every time I breathe. "I just need to get out of here."

She fumbles with her keys.

"Can you hurry, babe? They're sort of gonna be looking for me."

She drives, and I tell her what Mockler said.

"Jesus Christ!" She pounds on the steering wheel. "Charlotte just *told* him?"

"She . . . I don't know."

"She didn't even let you explain! She didn't even give you a fucking chance!"

It does seem like the least she could have done. And

she could have been there. . . . She didn't have to be so goddamn *sneaky*.

My chest is freezing.

"What a bitch," Naomi says.

"Nom, I'm aware! I'm aware that she's not perfect! What the fuck!"

Naomi throws her hands up. "Don't yell at me! I'm, like, the only person left on your side, remember?"

I hide my head in my palm. "Just drive."

"Where are we going?"

I swallow. *Think, Jonah.* I need to make things right. I need to get my happily ever after, with or without Charlotte. It's got to happen. I've got to make it happen.

"Work," I say. "Video store."

She squints. "Seriously?"

"Just do it. I need to talk to Max."

Naomi makes it to the parking lot much faster than Charlotte ever did. The jingle when I open the door does not help my headache.

Antonia scurries off Max's lap. God, there are customers here. Can't they wait? Do they have to shove this in everyone's faces?

"I need to talk to you," I say.

Max stands up. "Jonah, sit down."

"No, I can't. We need to talk. I'm in a hurry."

"You look awful. Sit down."

Antonia stands up and takes his elbow. "He's limping."

"No, that's not . . . that's not important. Max, listen, I need . . . some kind of escape, some way to get out of it, one of the happy movies—"

Max puts his hands up and backs away slowly, like I'm turning into a werewolf. "Jonah, maybe you should leave."

"No, I'm not—"

All the customers are staring at me.

"What?" I yell. "I'm not crazy! I'm not fucking crazy!"

Antonia says, "Jonah, leave!"

The next thing I know I'm outside, the night is black and long and cold, and Naomi says, "Home, Jonah, we have to go home," and it sounds like the worst and best thing anyone's ever told me all rolled into one.

twenty-five

THE PSYCHOLOGIST'S NAME IS DR. SCHNEIDER. It's written in curlicue letters on her door.

The couch is lavender plush and smells like roses. I sink back and am reminded of Charlotte. The white-noise machine wails like arctic wind.

After we've finished small-talking through my social life, school, work, and my dreams and aspirations, she says, "What's your family like?"

Dr. Schneider has a pretty green sweater and pointy glasses. I like her, but I hate being here.

I do my good-boy smile. "We make the Brady Bunch look like they need counseling."

She brushes her hair back. "That's not what I've heard."

My smile dims. "Which is?"

"That you've got a pretty sick little brother."

I twist my hands in my lap. I want Jesse beside me so badly that it hurts. "Okay. Yeah. We're messed up. I've got parents that should be divorced. But instead, they had a new baby, like Jesse wasn't already too much for them."

"Jesse's your brother?" His name sounds different coming from her—harsher, more metallic. It's not mean or ugly, but it's stronger than I'm used to hearing his name.

"Yes. My oldest brother. He's already a huge responsibility for my parents, and he needs to be a priority, but instead they've got this new baby. Who won't stop crying. Honestly. He cries all the time."

"Well—"

"And Jesse. Jesse is allergic to *everything*. Like, actually everything. And now that there's breast milk and baby formula and all this other crap he's allergic to, it's all over the house, and he can barely breathe. It's getting really bad. He's getting really bad."

"Do you worry about him a lot?"

I look down at my lap and nod, and then I'm crying so quickly and quietly that I didn't even feel it happen.

She gives me a minute, then passes me the tissue box.

"Want to talk about it?" she says.

I can't talk. I feel like my brain is squeezing through my sinuses. "I don't want to be here," I say.

"I know."

She looks like she really does know. Like maybe, back before she was a shrink, when she was just a person, maybe her parents or her principal made her come to a counselor, even though she didn't really need to. Maybe she once knew how it feels to not be messed up when you know you're supposed to be messed up. Maybe she can still remember it now.

I get a hold of myself. "He almost died twice this week," I say. "My fault. I just don't know how to take care of him."

"How old is he?"

"Sixteen. Less than a year and a half younger than me." I rub my nose. "My parents wanted a new kid right after me because I was crazy-easy. And then we had Jess, and he was all hospitalized and feeding tubed and didn't sleep through the night until he was five."

"Jonah?"

"It probably would have been earlier, except I kept waking him to make sure he was okay. I do all these stupid things because I think they'll help him, but I don't know what I'm doing."

"Jonah."

"He's stopped eating completely now. He hasn't eaten in almost a week."

"Jonah. What about your other brother?"

"He's eight months old. Eight and a half."

"What's his name?"

"Will."

I bite my lips. Everything's silent, save the white-noise whoosh.

"He cries a lot," I volunteer. "We don't know why. Jesse thinks it's food allergies. I think it's ear infections."

She keeps watching, like we're playing $10,000 Pyramid and she's waiting for the code word.

"Do you worry about him, too?" she eventually asks.

"Yes."

"You worry a lot, don't you?"

I know where this is going; it's going into nightmares and stress management and depression, and I shake my head very hard. "I *should* worry about them," I say.

"I understand."

"They need to be worried about. See." I swallow. "See, that's why it's so ironic that I'm here. I'm actually the only one in my family that's not, like, really, really messed up. But none of them—see, Jess is screwed and the baby's screwed, but it's not their fault. And there's nobody out there who can stop my damn parents. So they haul me in here instead and try to fix me because they can't fix my family."

"Who's 'they'?"

"Hmm?"

"Who's dragging you in here?"

I shrug. "The principal. My parents. Charlotte. Everyone but Naomi and Jesse."

She folds her hands. "I noticed your mother didn't come with you today."

"Yeah, she had to stay home and watch Jesse."

"And the baby?"

"Right."

She straightens her glasses. "Jonah. Do you realize how much you talk about him?"

"Talk about who?"

"Jesse."

Now I just want her to stop saying his name.

All I can think to say is, "He's important."

"I know, Jonah." She leans forward on her knees. "The heart of the matter, kid, is that you're here because you're hurting yourself. Drastically. And if I can't figure out why you're doing this, and how I can help you, we're going to have to consider checking into a facility so you can get some help."

My throat hurts. "You know about how broken bones grow back stronger?"

"Jonah."

"I won't do it again. It was stupid and selfish, I know."

"Jonah, listen." She gathers her red hair into a clip. "If there's anything I've figured out about you, it's that you're not selfish. And I have a really hard time believing that you'd do something so intense for any sort of selfish reason."

"I did. It is selfish." I start crying again. I'm always like this. Once I've broken down once, it doesn't take anything for me to get all weepy again.

She sighs, picks up her pad and pen, and starts to write.

"No, what are you writing?" I choke. "Please don't send me away."

She stops writing and watches me.

"Look." I scrub off the tears. "I didn't break my bones. My parents did it. I'm covering for them."

She shakes her head. "Jonah."

"Don't take me away from Jesse. I need to . . . I've got to take care of him. I've got to."

She says, "You just told me you didn't know how to take care of him."

I wail and sink my head onto my knees. I wonder if my dad can hear me out in the waiting room.

"Jonah. Do you feel guilty?"

I nod very hard.

"For being healthy?"

Now I stop.

She fixes her glasses. "Are you trying to be even with Jesse?"

I shake my head so much I think my neck will break. "I could never be as bad off as Jesse."

"Do you wish you could be?"

"No. No no no no. That would be awful. Please, please don't pass me off as one of those attention-seeking kids. It's not that. Really. I would never, *ever* want to be Jesse."

"Then what do you want?"

"I want to get better." Mucus drips all the way down to my upper lip, and I'm too broken to do anything about it. "That's the point."

"You really want to get better?"

I nod, then I realize with horror that we're talking about different things.

"No," I say. "Wait."

She's already writing. "This is nothing permanent, Jonah. You're not crazy. You're obviously a very bright boy."

"Stop it. Stop writing."

"Your parents have already expressed . . . interest in putting you under observation. It wouldn't be for long. A week at most."

I can fail chemistry in a week. I could lose Charlotte completely. Jesse could die of starvation, easily.

"I can't go away right now."

She looks at me for a long, long time. I do my best to look sane.

"We have to figure out why you're doing this, Jonah. I've got a place in mind for you. It's all teenagers, all short-term care. It'll be a lot like staying in a hospital." She nods toward my cast. "Which you've obviously experienced."

I try to smile, because this isn't her fault.

"It'll be okay," she says.

I croak, "All right."

At least I'll get out of that house.

"I'll call today, and see if they have a space," she says. "They'll probably be able to admit you tomorrow or the next day. Until then, will you take care of yourself? Can I trust you to do that?"

I nod. "So for now I get to go home?"

"Uh-huh. You go home and see your brothers, okay?"

I look at her sympathetic eyes behind those glasses and my whole throat hurts.

"It'll be all right," she says. "You'll even be out for Halloween."

The worst part is the car ride home. I try to sleep in the back, but Dad keeps looking at me in the rearview mirror. Eventually he calls home and spends about five minutes trying to shake Jesse off the phone. I hear Jesse freaking out, hear him asking questions—asking my father what's going to happen to me. Am I going to be okay. All the questions I always asked about him.

Dad gets rid of him and hooks Mom on the phone. They have a whispered, angry conversation—Dad says "I know I know I know," over and over again.

twenty-six

I GET HOME AND CRASH UNTIL TWO AND AFTERWARD
I want to get out, but Mom and Dad don't want me to
leave the house. They want to be there for me! They want
to talk! Dad even stayed home from work, just for lucky
old me.

They tell me to sit down on the couch next to them,
to curl up with some game shows. To let my brain mush
in sync with theirs.

But they don't meet my eyes when they ask me.

"I've got to talk to Charlotte." I'm wearing this old
gray T-shirt that's too small, and it pulls my shoulders
when I try to shrug. "I've got to try to fix things some-
what before I go away."

Dad's dressed down for the first time in weeks, and it just makes him look more uncomfortable. "Jonah, why don't you stay here? It's your last day home. Don't you want to be here when Jess gets back from school?"

God, they really don't get it at all.

I feel like saying, Are you kidding? Why would I want to see Jesse? When have I ever shown any interest in Jesse? Just to see how they'd react.

Instead, I beg. "Come on. Charlotte's a good influence. She's the one who told Mockler in the first place, remember?"

Mom pulls his sleeve. "Let him go."

He whirls to her. "Damn it, Cara, do we have to do this now?"

They start yelling and I slip out the front door. No problem. All kids should have neglectful parents.

Kidding.

It's a bit of a walk from home to school, but it's not like I have any choice. I don't have Jesse to drive me. I'm not sure I'd let him, anyway.

I'm cold in my T-shirt and my sling, but it doesn't resonate. I look at all the houses, imagining the normal families who live inside. Imagine them making sandwiches, or calling relatives, or . . . I don't know what normal people do.

What the hell is wrong with me?

I never thought I was crazy before. But ever since Dr. Schneider I can't stop spiraling. . . . I mean, I always knew what I was doing was a little out-there, but I never actually thought I was crazy.

I really didn't think it.

Fuck, I just wanted to be strong. And now everyone thinks I'm a lunatic. Even Charlotte, and Naomi, and Jesse—people who are not supposed to think that I'm a lunatic.

The walking thing is horribly painful. I get dizzier and dizzier with each step. My toes throb—the left foot is starting to break the tape. I give up and stop at the nearest bus stop, and I feel like I'm trying to hide in the glass booth. Trying and failing.

There's fake white-rap music emanating from a nearby house, like a soundtrack.

My cell phone rings in stark realistic contrast. Piercing the bubble of my whatever.

It's Naomi. She's in my phone book as "IMOAN."

I say, "Hey."

Her voice is excited and close to the speaker. "Are they locking you up? Run away. Seriously. I had a cousin who got locked up."

"They're not locking me up." I wonder when the next

bus is coming. "I'm just going in for evaluation. For a few days. They'll realize I'm not crazy after, like, a day and I'll get to come home."

"Oh, yeah? And how are they going to realize that?"

"I'll tell them I'm not breaking anymore."

"Yeah. Okay. And they'll realize you're lying when you come into the infirmary in little pieces."

"Naomi. I'm not breaking anymore."

"What?"

"Stop it!" I kick my heels against the ground. My toes shake around like puzzle pieces. "This isn't working. I've ruined *everything*."

"Jonah."

"This was supposed to get him better."

These words freeze in the back of my throat.

Did I honestly just figure this out?

Naomi says, "Jesse? How was this supposed to help him?"

I close my eyes. "Forget it."

"You said this wasn't about him."

"I know! I fucking know what I said!"

No. I didn't just figure it out. I knew it. I always knew it.

Shit.

She doesn't speak. I can hear her breathing, all slow

and even, like this isn't the worst moment of my life. Like she really thinks staying calm is going to help me.

"You can't cure him," she whispers.

"I know that! You think I don't fucking know that? You think I need you to tell me that?"

"I'm just saying."

"No! Don't say it! I fucking know it, Naomi!"

The bus rolls up to the curb and the doors spring open. One is loose and wobbles back and forth in the breeze.

I gimp onto the bus and stick my phone in my pocket so I can drop a handful of change into the meter. I could probably get disabled fare, if I wanted, but I'm too damn tired to ask.

"He's generally okay," Naomi says as I retrieve the phone from my pocket.

"Yeah, generally."

"That's better than you are."

I sit down and put my head against the window, holding the cell away from my ear so she sounds very far away.

"Aren't you in class?" I say.

"School just ended."

"Where's Charlotte?"

"Don't know. Aren't you mad at her?"

I ignore this. "Seen Jess?"

"Yeah. He's in the weight room. Wouldn't talk much. I brought him an apple."

"Clean?"

"Of course. I'm not an idiot. But he didn't eat it."

The bus speeds up and all those damn houses start to blur. "I'm coming to school now."

"Seriously?"

"I've got to find Charlotte."

"She told on you."

"Yeah, I'm aware. That's why I've got to talk with her."

"She fucking betrayed you!"

"Yeah, because she's not an idiot. She found out I was breaking my own bones, Nom. What was she supposed to do?"

Naomi gets her pissed-off voice. "Uh, okay. So does that make me a crappy friend, or what?"

Basically. "Nom."

"I was being supportive. Friends are supposed to be supportive."

"Okay."

"No, don't 'okay' me. What should I have done?"

I swallow and look around the bus, but none of the other passengers even look conscious, let alone interested.

"You probably shouldn't have encouraged me to keep breaking when I wanted to stop."

"Jonah," she says, and her voice is back to kind.

I chew the inside of my mouth.

"What was I supposed to do? Let you think you could stop? And then let you fail?"

"I can stop."

"Okay," she says, and she's so quietly begging, so quietly . . . supportive. "Okay. I hope you're right."

twenty-seven

FIVE MINUTES LATER I DISMOUNT THE BUS, CROSS
to the school, and there she is, her shoes tip-tapping
through the parking lot on the way to her car.
"Charlotte."

She keeps walking. The daffodil in her bun looks like
it's crying.

"Charlotte, listen to me. Come on. I can't chase you."

She stops. Her shadow is small and sad on the pavement.

"I have to feed the cats," she whispers.

"Please."

She takes the teeniest little steps towards me, like this
can help her convince herself she's not really giving in.

"How are you?" she asks.

"I'm okay."

She swallows and looks down. "I heard you're getting help."

"Yeah. Please don't give me that speech, that sad look, okay? Listen, babe. I'm not crazy. I swear I'm not crazy."

She looks down, and I see her eyelashes are wet. She's not crying, though, not really; it's like her mascara has a mind of its own.

"I know how this works," she says. "I know the—okay. I've been doing research. Lots of people do—do what you're doing. It's just normally not so dramatic."

"That's not what this is." But I know how goddamn counterproductive this argument is getting, and I'm so sick of it. It doesn't matter why I did this, not anymore; the point is that I did it and now I have to deal with the consequences. I have to make it better.

I say, "I just don't want you to be afraid of me."

She's shaking. "I don't know if I can wait for you—"

"Damn it, Charlotte, I'm going to a psych ward, not jail. Not war."

"But—"

"Frankly, Charlotte, I don't give—"

"Don't do that."

"No. It's your fault I'm going, kid, because you didn't

wait long enough for me to explain this to you! You just went to Mockler. . . . Babe, you weren't even there when he confronted me! That's a low move. You're such a nice person—you *know* that wasn't nice."

She stares at the ground.

I say, "If you don't want to be with me because I'm crazy, just say it. I'm only going to be gone for, like, a week. Don't give me this waiting talk."

"I'm not with you!" She throws her arms in the air and her bracelets slide all the way down to her shoulders. "We're not dating, remember?"

"Oh, bullshit, Charlotte."

She pulls back like I hit her.

I imagine everyone in the parking lot holding their breath as I wait for her to speak.

"This isn't working," she says.

"What's not?"

"Nothing." She laughs, deep and sick. "I guess nothing isn't working. That's what this is, right?"

"Stop."

"I don't even know why you told me." She shrugs, faking heartless. "If I really don't mean *shit* to you, I don't know why you told me you did this yourself."

The word sounds especially foul from her mouth.

"I didn't tell you," I spit. "You forced it out of me."

I snap my mouth closed, like this will stop what I've already said.

"Well, then," she says under her breath.

Someone nearby lights a cigarette, and my mouth fuzzes with the candy-apple taste of the smoke.

I turn around and leave before she can stop me. Not that she would.

Students giggle as I walk through the parking lot. I don't know if they're laughing at me or if they're just happy, and I don't know which option would depress me more.

twenty-eight

IT'S ALMOST TIME TO LEAVE FOR THE CRAZY BIN,
but there's one thing left to do. At about six o'clock, I
take an apple from the refrigerator. I bring it to the sink
and scrub it so hard that it would bleed, if it were alive. Will
watches me, screaming while he sucks on his fingers.

I won't touch him right now.

I can hear Jess snoring from halfway down the hall.
Some stupid part of me doesn't want to wake him up.

Really stupid part.

I crack his door open. He's curled up on top of all his
blankets, his arms tucked underneath his chest. Every
snore gives away how stuffed-up he is.

"Jess." I put my hand on his back and work my fingers around his skinny ribs. "Wake up, kid."

He frees his hand and rubs his eyes. "Hey." He sees the apple. "What are you doing?"

"Sit up. I need to talk to you, all right?"

He rocks upright and wraps himself around his stomach. I sit down beside him and tuck him under my good arm.

"Okay?" I say.

He nods and buries his face in the armpit of my T-shirt. "Don't go away. Don't go away don't go away."

"Listen, Jess."

He keeps swallowing, and I can see it in his neck.

I shouldn't have woken him up.

"Don't worry about me while I'm gone," I say. "That's an order."

He croaks, "Okay."

"Look at me. Jesse, look at me."

He's crying a little bit and trying to hide it from me, which is stupid. His eyes are struck pink, and his tears are thick like spit.

I say, "I'm not going to be gone for long. I'll be back really soon. And you'll be fine until then. Really."

"Okay."

"If I hear you're in the hospital with a reaction while I'm gone, I'm gonna fucking kill you."

He cough-laughs.

"And if you come to my crazy-person place with some kind of eating disorder . . . that'll kill me, man."

He covers his cheeks with his hands. "I don't have an eating disorder."

"Jesse. Jesse, come on."

He puts his hands on his forehead. He's struggling not to cover his ears—that's what he does when he's really upset.

I make *shhh* noises.

"It's . . . I'm fucking terrified," he says.

"I know. I get it."

"I don't want another reaction."

"I know. But I don't want you to starve, either. It's been, like, five days since you've eaten."

He nods.

"You've got to feel awful."

He keeps nodding, like he doesn't know how to stop.

I say, "I'm not leaving if you don't eat. I'll kick and scream and they'll have to drag me away from here." I hold him more tightly. I'm his seat belt. "And then they probably won't let me out for a long, long time."

"Are you seriously blackmailing me?"

"Uh-huh." I hand him the apple. "It's totally clean.

You're not going to get sick. I'll stay here and watch you for a reaction if you want."

He stares at the apple. "Come home soon, okay?"

"I will. And you can come visit me."

"Okay."

"Seriously, now. Just eat the apple."

He stares at the skin for a long time, then tucks his lips between his teeth and shakes his head. "I don't want to."

"Don't care. I'm making you."

"Don't."

"I'll shove it down your fucking throat, Jesse." I stand up. "Eat it. Now."

He doesn't move, so I grab his scratchy jaw and force his mouth open. He coughs on me.

"Eat now. Eat the apple."

He doesn't move—doesn't fight, and doesn't lift the apple to his parted lips.

"I'm not giving up, here, Jesse. Eat."

When he latches his teeth around the apple, I let him go and watch him bite. All the terrible things I've ever done to him come back to me. The time I convinced him to come leaf-jumping with me and he swelled up like a sprained ankle. The time he was choking from an egg reaction and I just stood there with his EpiPen reading the directions because I couldn't remember how to give it to him. All the foods I'd given him that ended up making him sick. All the hives I'd ignored.

He chews and swallows.

"All right?" I say.

"Yeah."

He looks at me with drizzly eyes that are somewhere between angry and grateful.

I try to ignore it all. "Okay. Listen . . . take care of Mom and Dad. Don't touch Will. Let the parents worry about him, okay?"

Jesse swallows and takes another bite.

"And don't let them make you too crazy," I add. "Remember that whole family thing, okay?"

"You and your Confucianism."

"It's important."

He says okay and I hug him.

"Don't think I'm leaving until you've finished that," I say, and I don't. He finishes.

twenty-nine

THE RANDELLY CARE HOME DOESN'T LOOK LIKE home at all. It's just another name for a hospital building, and it's brown and hides behind a grove of cherry trees, like this will help it go away.

Dad carries my duffel bag. Mom hits the buzzer on the door and identifies us. We're admitted with this awful grinding noise.

Yeah. They're both out of the house at the same time. They left Jesse with the baby, which is the worst idea ever right now.

"The waiting room's lovely," Mom says, examining the curtain and the upholstery. The room's been sprayed so heavily with lemon air freshener that I can taste it and feel it between my teeth.

Dad and I slug up to the front desk. "This is Jonah McNab," he says. "He's here for evaluation."

I wonder who wrote that little speech for him.

The girl behind the desk wears a volunteer polo and has matching barrettes in her hair. She couldn't be older than eighteen. But still, you've got to wonder what kind of person wants to volunteer here. Probably a little nuts herself.

She makes that study-me-like-she's-not-studying-me thing.

"Hi," I say. "I'm Jonah."

Dad looks at me like I'm not supposed to speak. Like I've broken the law of the crazies.

She doesn't. She just smiles. "I'm Mackenzie. You're going to be in room 215, Jonah. That's second floor, all right? Elevator's there, and the doctor should be in to speak with you and run you through inspection within the hour."

"Okay. Thank you."

I walk with Mom and Dad over to the elevators. When the doors swish open, a boy's already in there. He's barefoot and wearing pajamas. He looks normal, if a little high-strung.

He nods at me when I walk on, then he eyes my parents. "New kid?" he says through the side of his mouth, like a spy.

I nod.

"Welcome to the clan."

Well. I've always liked clans.

Mom and Dad look at each other, pissed-off-worried. Yeah, parents, I get it. They don't want me associating with these kids, but . . . do they really expect me not to talk to anyone the whole time I'm here?

"What room are you?" the boy asks.

"215."

He nods. "I'm 212. Stop by sometime."

My room's just off the elevator and to the left. The boy stops a few doors before me, hits it with his hip, and goes inside.

Dad puts his hand on my back as he opens my door.

The bed and desk are nailed to the floor, but there is threadbare carpet and a drippy radiator and a closet—it's not a prison. The bedsprings squeak when I sit down.

"No roommate," Dad says. "That'll be nice."

I shrug.

Mom sits down beside me and holds my hand. "Do you want us to stay until the doctor comes?"

"No. Please don't. I want you to be home in case the baby wakes up."

"Jesse can get him."

Dad says, "Jesse should not be touching the baby, Cara."

Mom stares into my face like she's expecting something more.

"I kind of do want to be alone," I say.

Dad chews the inside of his lips, and Mom keeps watching me, her cheeks shaking in that about-to-cry face.

It's insensitive and awful of me, but I get so fucking pissed off when my Mom cries. It's just never what I want to see. It doesn't *help*.

"I'll be fine." I hold my hair.

Mom wipes a minuscule tear off her eye. "We'll come visit every day."

I hug them good-bye. Dad holds me and puts his hand on the back of my head in this totally way-affectionate-not-Dad way. "You're a good boy," he says. "You're going to be fine."

Once they're gone, my stomach feels gross and empty. I take a handful of strawberries out of my backpack and eat them while I put my clothes away, but it doesn't really help.

I wonder if they're going to confiscate my strawberries.

"Hey, new kid?"

I bring my head out of the closet. The boy from the elevator and a chubby blond girl stand at my doorway.

"Hey," I say.

He jerks his head to the side. "You want to hang out? We're all in the lounge. I'm Tyler. This is Annie."

She waggles her fingers.

"I'm Jonah," I say, trailing down the hallway behind them.

"Good," Tyler calls over his shoulder. He takes one of my strawberries.

We walk down the hall, away from the elevators, pass door after door. Most of the rooms look cold and empty; I guess October isn't a popular month for crazy kids.

"They let the boys and girls stay on the same floor?" I ask.

Tyler says, "There's only one floor. I guess they assume we're too fucked up to get it on. Though the stains on my mattress suggest otherwise." Strawberry juice drips down his chin.

At the end of the hall there's a wide room with two propped-open doors. Four kids sit around in armchairs, throwing playing cards onto the floor.

"Hey," Tyler says. "Look what I brought. New kid."

Most of them wear sweatpants and socks, and I know

I overpacked. One of the girls pulls Tyler onto her lap and gives him a few cards. Annie sits on the floor, picks up the pile of cards in front of her, and hands them to me.

I edge to the floor beside her. "Thank you."

She nods.

They all look like regular kids who got squeezed out. Empty teenage tubes of toothpaste. It's not that bad.

"We're letting Mariah win," Tyler says. "Because she's going home today."

"They're not letting me win." Mariah has lime green toenails and wears more makeup than the rest of the girls combined. She shifts Tyler over on her lap and hides her cards from him. "I'm just full of mad skills."

I make an awkward smile.

"You better be spelling that with a *z*," Tyler says.

She wrinkles her nose. "Like . . . *skillz*?"

"Exactly."

"Only you, babe." She turns to me. "When'd you get here?"

I look at my cards. Nine of clubs, four of spades, six of spades, queen of hearts. "Like, five minutes ago."

Tyler leans his head against Mariah's. "His parents were so middle-American."

"Mariah was trying to stay here longer than me." This slack-face guy with a bit of a beard and a haunted voice throws two cards into the center pile. "But nobody can. I'm out."

Tyler says, "You're hiding cards in your pocket."

He sighs and takes them out.

"And stop complaining, Stephen."

He sorts his cards. "I'm just saying. It's been three weeks."

"If you stopped sneaking in candles, they'd probably let you go home."

"I'm not burning," he mumbles. "I just like candles."

"Yeah, but they see a burner with candles . . . and they think you're burning."

I feel almost like laughing. He's been here three weeks for burning himself. . . . I'll probably be here for fucking months. I guess I'll have to avoid sneaking in sledgehammers or skateboards.

This skinny-skinny girl from the corner reaches out and takes all the cards from the middle. "We're gonna miss you, Mariah."

"Shh." The brunette next to the skinny girl captures her under her arm. It reminds me of me and my father at Jesse's hockey game, and I look away.

Tyler flicks through his hand. "Leah, I don't know if you should have taken those cards."

Skinny girl says, "I needed them."

"That's hardly letting me win, though." Mariah taps her green fingernails over her lips. "Oops."

Annie drops some cards into the pile.

Tyler says, "Wanna go, Jonah?"

"I don't know how to play."

He shakes his head. "Just play, man."

I flick the six of spades into the middle. I'm rewarded with a host of approving nods.

Everyone plays. Tyler throws down the rest of his hand. "I lose."

On my turn, I take all the cards.

Everyone applauds, and Tyler smiles. "Yeah, man, you're gonna fit in just fine."

I'll take this as a compliment.

thirty

"THOUGHTS OF SUICIDE IN THE PAST WEEK?"

I shake my head. The doctor shoves his glasses up his beaked nose and pulls his chair closer to my bed. From my experience, I can conclude that all doctors wear glasses. This guy. Dr. Schneider. The ER docs. Even Jesse's immunologist.

I can't picture Will's pediatrician, but I assume he wears glasses too.

"Taken any drugs?" he asks. "Alcohol?"

"In the past week?"

He glances up from his clipboard. His eyes look crossed from behind those enormous lenses. His cologne is the same stuff my math teacher wears, and I'm drowning in the sweaty pepper smell.

I run the bed sheet between my fingers. "No. No drugs or alcohol."

One beer on Naomi's car doesn't count, right?

"Have you hurt yourself in the past week?"

I nod.

"Are you in any pain right now?"

"Uh-uh." Just my head and my damn toes, but none of it feels real enough to mention.

"All right, then . . ." He snaps a bracelet around my wrist. "We're going to have you in for counseling once a day after lunch, all right? You'll be expected to check in for meals three times a day. Most activities will be downstairs. One of your friends can show you the way."

Friends?

"Your curfew is eleven—make sure you're in your room. One of the volunteers will check your vitals before bed and when you wake up. There'll be nurses around all day and all night if you need anything."

"Okay."

"There are activities during the day—arts and crafts, exercise time. You'll have to report to those. And that's really it."

"So . . . what do I do the rest of the time?"

He fiddles with his sleeves. I think he's more

uncomfortable than I am. "Keeping a journal can help. You'll have visits from your family. Maybe a close friend."

I imagine Charlotte here, but I know it's just a dream. "I don't have to be doing anything?"

"No. This isn't a jail, Jonah. You're here for observation and diagnosis, not punishment. You can keep your cell phone, some comforts from home. You're free most of the day to relax, talk to the other kids. We believe this time for self-reflection will be useful, and that it can motivate one another to get better. Our goal here is to lead you toward self-sufficiency, and that's why our rules here are simple—take care of yourself, and support the other residents as they work toward their recovery. But you'll have access to doctors or nurses all the time, if you need anything, and they'll have access to you."

He shakes my hand and wishes me a speedy recovery, and I'm so fucking tired. I'm halfway under the blanket when a girl appears in my doorway. She pauses, her toe pointed in the beginnings of a step.

"Sorry," she says. "Do you want to be alone?"

She's dressed like someone from the real world, and I realize it's Mackenzie, the volunteer from the front desk.

I scoot into the open air. "No, come in."

She waves a blood-pressure cuff. "Just here for your vitals. They like to know what you're at when you come in."

"Okay."

She wraps the cuff around my good arm and starts to pump it up. "How you feeling today?"

"Okay."

"Homesick at all? Do you need anything?"

"I'll be all right. My family's coming to see me tomorrow."

She nods. "Your parents looked nice."

"They are." Nice isn't the problem.

"Siblings?"

"Two little brothers."

"I'm an only child. Always wanted siblings. Are they a handful?"

I smile. "Mine are."

She stops talking and deflates the cuff, counting seconds on her watch.

"Eighty-two over fifty. You're really not stressing, are you?"

"I'm not the stress type."

She studies me, head tilted to the side. "How many broken bones do you have? If you don't mind my asking . . ."

"Eighteen, right now, if you count toes."

"Man. How'd that happen?"

I wonder what it'd be like to explain this all to someone who's never met Jesse.

She keeps her eyes on me, but I just smile and say, "It's kind of a long story."

She smiles back. "Well, maybe you'll tell me someday. You've got arts and crafts at three thirty, okay? Downstairs, off the lobby to the left. Don't be late."

"Okay, thanks."

Mackenzie pauses at my door. "Let me know if you need anything."

I fall asleep on my bed and dream about Charlotte. She's telling me something, but I can't hear over the damn baby.

thirty-one

TYLER POUNDS HIS PILE OF PLAY-DOH INTO submission. "I hate arts and crafts," he mumbles, shaking the table with his smacks. "Arts and crafts is bullshit."

Annie, next to me, doodles thousands of cottages with smoke uncurling from the chimneys.

Leah's wrist is about as big around as her paintbrush. "You're just pissed Mariah's gone."

"No, I'm not." Tyler carves the Play-Doh with his fingernail. "I'm just pissed."

"You loved her."

The art room is wicked bright and smells like clay. A sink runs continuously by the window. The kiln sits open, a fake-me-out suicide oven. "I know you wouldn't, and what's cool is you couldn't fit in there anyway," Stephen mumbled to me when we came in, and it scares me how well he gets me.

Tyler says, "I didn't love her. I don't like girls. I told you."

"Rrrright."

"I don't."

Stephen comes over and observes our progress. "Very good," he says, like he's our teacher. "Now, Jonah, why aren't you arting and crafting?"

"I don't know what to do."

He throws me a mound of clay.

Our real teacher is a big woman with wiry hair who reads a romance novel in the corner. Every once in a while she shouts out something inspirational. "You kids are doing great!" and "Keep it up." "Feel the healing." This place is such a joke.

I wonder what healing really feels like.

The walls are covered in dirty blue wallpaper that's probably supposed to make me feel calm. It works.

I start shaping the clay into a tree. "This is kind of hard one-handed."

"So what happened to you?" Stephen says. "Were you in some kind of accident?"

I shake my head.

"I bet he did it himself." Tyler nudges Amy. "You did it yourself, didn't you, Jonah?"

The brunette, Belle, says, "You don't have to sound so fucking enthusiastic."

"It's hard-core. I'm appreciative of his hard-coreness." Tyler raises his eyebrows at me. "So you did do it yourself, right?"

Ah, what the hell. "Yeah."

"Intense."

"It wasn't like that."

"Man, I know." Tyler slaps my good shoulder. "It's never like that."

"No, I mean, it's not a suicide-type thing. It's not even a self-injury thing. It's not like that. I'm not depressed." I stand up my tree trunk and start adding branches.

"I'm manic-depressive," Tyler says.

Leah says, "It's 'bipolar,' now, Ty."

"Fuck that. I like manic-depressive. Belle's depressed, unlike you. Leah's obviously anorexic."

She smiles at me.

"Stephen's a burner, and Annie doesn't talk."

"I talk," she whispers.

Tyler looks at me, his voice gently urgent. "And you're what, then?"

"I'm . . . an obsessive self-improver." I make leaves.

"Looks more like self-destruction to me."

I shrug at Belle. "They're similar."

Stephen smiles. "Yeah. Yeah, they are."

"You get hurt, you grow back stronger," I say.

"Yeah." Stephen nods, his grin widening. "Yeah. Yeah, you do."

I feel all warm and soft inside despite the air conditioning and the lemon pledge. It's this comfort of being understood.

"You're doing great, kids," the teacher says, and we all turn back to our art projects. Even Tyler. A slow smile spreads across his face.

thirty-two

THAT NIGHT, I TRY TO SLEEP.

"It's going to be hard," Tyler warned me earlier. "You'll have a really rough time with it the first night."

I thought he was crazy. I never have a hard time sleeping. If I can sleep through the baby noise, I can sleep through anything, right?

Right?

I've got a blanket of Will's and a picture of Mom and Dad and one of Jesse's hockey pucks. I've spread them out on my dresser, like a shrine to my misery.

I'm sitting on the edge of my bed, my arms around my stomach, wondering if I'm going to throw up. Or if my appendix is about to burst or something.

In true melodramatic fashion, there's a storm out-side. I don't mind the thunder, but the quiet moments in between drill into my skull. If silence could break bones, I would shatter right now, into pieces of stomachache and blueprints and desperation.

I pull on some socks and pad down the hall. The nau-sea fades the farther I get from my bed. I tap on Tyler's door and call his name, softly.

He opens up, his hands over his lips like he's about to yawn, or cough. But he doesn't do either.

I shake and stamp my feet against the ground to remind me where I am. My toes hate this.

"You've gotta stop," Tyler says. "One of the nurses will come. They'll hear you up."

I'm so, so cold.

"Just tell me everything's okay," I say.

"Everything's okay, Jonah."

"You're okay?"

"I'm okay."

"And everything's okay?"

"Yeah. I promise."

Tyler guides me back to my room. My stomachache is starting to ebb, and I feel content in this quiet way.

Maybe because it's so. Quiet.

No coughing and snoring and wheezing from stuffed-up Jesse. No parents screaming at each other, or baby screaming back.

Just me.

Here.

Dark room.

Cold mattress.

Cold Jonah.

I sing just to make noise until I finally fall asleep.

thirty-three

AND MY BOY HIMSELF STICKS HIS HEAD THROUGH my door at about four the next afternoon, two days before Halloween. "Knock knock," he says, like a little geek.

"Jesse!" I drop my book and leap on him. "You're not supposed to be up here!"

"I snuck up. There's crappy security in this place, you know that? You could totally just come home if you wanted." He disentangles himself from my hug and holds me at arm's length. "How the hell are you, brother?"

"I'm okay. You look . . . fuck, you look fantastic."

He smiles. "I'm pretty good."

He has color and clear eyes and no hives. He's got

a sad mouth but his lips aren't swollen. So he looks incredible.

"Have you been living at home?"

He laughs. "Yeah. It's just been a good day."

"You're eating," I say.

"Yeah, I'm eating."

"That's good, man." I slap him on the back. "Glad to hear it."

"I knew you would be."

On the way to the elevator, we run into Tyler and Stephen. "Guys," I say. "This is my brother."

Tyler says, "What's up, man?" Neither he nor Stephen is a hand-shaking kind of guy, which saves Jesse his usual awkward I-can't-touch-you explanation.

Jess smiles as we head toward the elevator. He has his hands in his pockets and kicks the linoleum. He's nervous, but more politely than Mom and Dad were. "This isn't so bad."

"Nah, it isn't. I should kidnap you for the weekend and you can crash with me. My room's big enough."

"Yeah, hopefully you won't be here long enough to consider that."

I hit the down button. "So how's shit at home?"

He shrugs. "Not awful, actually. Naomi's over all the time. She misses you. I think Will does too. He's even louder than usual. Mom and Dad both came, you know. Got a sitter. I wanted to bring him, but Mom and Dad still don't want him outside."

"Heard from Charlotte?"

He makes his I'm-sorry face and shakes his head.

"She'll come around," I say.

"Of course she will." He squeezes my shoulder. "No doubt, man."

Leah gets onto the elevator with us just before the doors close. Anyone thicker than her probably would have gotten stuck. "Who's this?" she says.

"This is Jesse. My little brother."

"Nice to meet you," she says.

He's so cute around pretty girls. "Nice to meet *you*." He points at the buttons, his cheeks getting pink like he's a cartoon. "What's on the third floor?"

"Don't know," I say. "We never go up there."

Leah says, "I have it on good authority that's where they do the electroshock therapy."

I elbow her. "Don't scare him."

He scoffs. "I'm not scared." As we walk off the elevator and part ways with Leah, he mumbles, "She seems nice."

"You could get with her, no problem. She's nice and clean. Doesn't eat."

"I don't want her. She's way too skinny."

Mom and Dad sit in armchairs by the doors, like they're afraid to venture too far inside. They've dressed up. I appreciate Jesse extra hard, in his dirty jeans and T-shirt.

"Hey," I say, and hug them.

"How was your first night?" Mom won't stop touching me—my arm, my face, my hair, like she hasn't seen me since I was a kid.

"It was fine. You don't have to worry about me. I'm really fine here." I smile at Belle as she walks through the lobby, cuddling some tiny stuffed bear into her chest.

"Do you know her?" Dad asks, and he says it more gently than I expect.

"There're only, like, six other kids here. I sort of know everyone."

"What are they like?" Mom asks.

"They're fine. Really. Everything's fine."

"When can you come home?" Jess says.

My tongue expands with pity and fills my whole mouth, and I can't talk.

Dad examines my pajama pants and ratty T-shirt. "Do you need more clothes?"

I manage to swallow. "No, no, I'm fine."

"How's the doctor?"

"He's all right. We had our first session this afternoon. Doesn't talk about much. He mostly just makes me put together puzzles and watches me and stuff. It's like ADD testing."

Jesse sneezes a few times and I look at him sideways.

"Everything's okay," I say. "We have art every day. And we play basketball outside."

Jesse's red ears twitch up. "Basketball?"

"Uh-huh. I mean, I'm mostly just limping around, but . . . it's cool. And I've got lots of books. How's school?"

Jesse smiles. "Mr. Roskull got a toupee."

"You're kidding."

"It's *disgusting*."

"The counselor spoke with Jesse," Mom says. "Wanted to know how you're doing."

Jess swipes his nose. "And I told her you were fine. Which he is. I saw his room. He hasn't torn up the walls or bled everywhere. Look at him." He waves his hand from the top of my head to my shoes. "No new broken bones. He's fine. Bring him home."

Dad looks at the floor. "Jonah, you understand—"

"Yeah, I do. Stop, Jess."

He's tearing up, and I can't tell if he's crying or it's allergies. "I don't believe this."

"Calm down."

Mom and Dad just sit there, bouncing their eyes between Jesse and me.

He starts coughing.

"Look, take him home," I say, my stomach hurting. "They air-freshen like crazy here. It isn't good for him. He shouldn't be here."

Jess clears his throat. "I'm okay."

Yeah, he was okay before he got here. But now . . . it's not like I think he's on the brink of death, but his voice is stuffed up and his eyes are getting red and those throat-clearing noises are just too hard to listen to. He can't belong here. He can't belong at home, and he can't belong here. He can't belong anywhere I am.

"Look at him," I say. "He needs to get out of here."

Mom and Dad gather their coats, and I pull Jesse to the side to say good-bye. "Come home," he says.

"I will. Look," I say, and my voice goes all on its own. "Come visit on your own, okay? So we won't have to deal with them. And we'll stay outside." I fish a tissue out of my pocket and hand it to him. "More fresh air, less air freshener."

He laughs, and his throat sounds wet. "Okay. Look . . . please get home ASAP. We need you, all right?"

"You're doing great. Look at you."

He shakes his head. "I don't care. Come home."

Yeah, but I care, you idiot. *Someone* has to look out for you.

They all trample out, Jesse behind with his hands in his pockets, and I collapse into one of the armchairs. Mackenzie watches me from the desk.

Tyler perches on a chair beside me. "Was that your brother?"

"Yeah."

"Hmm." He stretches his legs out. "He didn't look sick."

"Yeah, I know." I nod. "He might be better without me."

"Don't say that."

"Trust me." I push my hair back. "I don't want to." But I'm running out of other options.

thirty-four

STEPHEN SAYS, "COME ON OUT. WE'RE HAVING A crazy-kid party." He clings to my door like it's all that's keeping him standing.

"Mmmm." I put my hands in my hair. "I don't really feel like it."

"You've been in your room for hours."

What am I supposed to say? I've been sick to my stomach ever since Mom and Dad and Jesse left.

Stephen sits at the foot of my bed. "Leah says your brother's cute."

"Yeah. He's good-looking when he's healthy." I stretch my legs out. "I just . . . I don't know if I should go home."

"Like now?"

"Like when they let me out."

"What are you talking about?"

"My brother. He never looked that good when I was at home."

"You can't seriously think that your being here is making him better. You've been here for, like, a day. And aren't you guys close?"

I shrug, because "close" isn't exactly the word.

He shakes his head slowly. "Come into the lounge."

"I'm not feeling really social."

"Yeah. You're depressed. You think we don't know depressed? Come on, Jonah."

I pull on a pair of socks and follow Stephen to the lounge. All the chairs are abandoned and everyone's crashed on the floor, flopped on top of one another in a big teenage pile.

"Hey, Jonah," they chorus.

I crawl into the mess and rest my head on Belle's shoulder. She pats it like I'm a good dog, and I think about Charlotte.

"Tyler's telling us a story," she says.

Tyler shifts. "So, yeah . . . that's kind of why I hate my stepfather. I kind of blame him."

"You can't blame him for your going psycho," Leah says.

"What, and you don't hate anyone for your . . . you know."

"Of course not. It's my fault. No one made me stop eating."

Belle's shirt rides up and I see all the cuts above her hips. My stomach turns flip-flops.

"What about you, Jonah?" someone, everyone asks.

I close my eyes and tell them about the car accident, and after the car accident, and after after the car accident. . . .

They all suck in their breath.

"That sounds fucking awful." Tyler rolls onto his stomach.

"It's sort of hard to remember the really bad parts." Of the accident. Of all of it.

He says, "Doesn't it hurt? Breaking your bones?"

Talking about it is this weird type of freedom. "Totally, yeah, but there is that adrenaline rush."

Stephen nods.

"So that's why you do it?" Tyler says.

I laugh. "I don't know if I should be giving you guys any self-injury motivations."

They laugh too.

"Come on, Jonah."

I shake my head.

Tyler concedes. "But you do have a reason, right?"

"Yeah. Oh, definitely have a reason." I stare up at the ceiling. My heart throbs as I breathe. "I just didn't always know what it was."

Belle squeezes me.

I'm in my room by curfew, but the rest of everybody is wandering the halls. Some nurse starts yelling, and they yell right back. I smile into my Confucius biography.

"Good day?"

I look up and Mackenzie's grinning at me, blood-pressure cuff dangling from one hand.

"It got better kind of suddenly."

She tightens the cuff, then lets it go. I'm aware of my heartbeat again. She says, "Eighty over fifty. Still low. Are you sick? You're kind of pale."

I shake my head. "Feel like listening?"

She sits cross-legged at the foot of my bed. "It is in my job description."

"I saw my little brother today, and just . . . I don't know. Started thinking." I pick up my book. "Do you know anything about Confucianism?"

She shakes her head.

"Oh. Well, I'm kind of into it. Anyway, there's this idea—the main idea, actually. It's that the family is the smallest possible unit of measurement. Like, you can't divide a family into the individuals. Not really. Because every decision, every problem . . . it's all within the family. It's all shared. You're born, and you're born into part of this organism. You're like parts of a cell, working to make the whole thing better."

She says, "You can kind of divide everything into that."

"What?"

"Oh, I don't know. Family. Friends. School." She shrugs. "Here. You're always a part of something. It's never just you. Anyway. You were talking."

"It's okay." I tighten my lower jaw, and the wire pulls. "For me . . . see, I've got this really sick little brother."

"Oh."

"I don't want to make it sound like this is all about him, like he's messed me up or something. And I don't want to make it sound like this is sudden. He's sixteen now. . . . He's been sick since he was born. But he's done all he can to keep himself healthy. He avoids what he's allergic to, and he works out all the time, and he tries to have a normal life, like, he tries really hard. He does all he can to make himself stronger. He's reached his limit. He's done his part—for himself, for the whole family unit."

"He can't get well?"

I shake my head. "No cure."

"That's awful."

I swallow. "Okay. But. If our family is really the smallest unit, then every time Jesse's sick, we're all sick. His pain is our pain. So if he can't get better . . ." I wave my broken wrist. "I'm the next best thing. I get hurt, and I heal. And I get stronger. And my strength is Mom's strength. Is Dad's strength. Is Jesse's strength."

"That's . . ."

"I know it's kind of crazy."

"It's adorable, Jonah."

I rest my chin on my knees. "I miss him."

My eyes flick toward my door and there's Tyler, Belle, Leah, and Annie, their mouths all popped open in surprise. Or understanding.

thirty-five

WHEN I REPEAT THIS EXPLANATION TO THE psychologist the next day, he's less impressed.

"But, Jonah," he says. "It doesn't make *sense*."

Small-minded Western thinkers.

"There's got to be something else you can do, if you want to support your family," he says. "Something that doesn't involve self-injury."

"I try," I insist.

"I know you do."

"No, you don't."

I stare above at the wall over his ergonomic chair. The clock on the wall is exactly the same shape as his head, but the face is less serious. More interesting.

I wait until I'm calm enough to speak, and I say, "I've tried everything."

"I know it must look like—"

"No. I've tried everything."

"Breaking your bones is obviously not the answer, Jonah."

"Yeah. I'm aware. I'm aware that it didn't work."

"So what's your new plan?"

This is a snide question, so I don't tell him about how I have to leave my family organism, break out firmly and finally. I don't tell him that I'm a parasite, and I'm ruining them. That my functionality is tearing them to pieces.

He doesn't deserve to know. And it's not as if I want to talk about it.

He's back to his shrink speech. "The trouble with self-injury is that you develop a pattern of behavior. It's not enough to simply say that you're going to stop hurting yourself. What we need to do is construct an alternate outlet—a separate pattern of behavior that you follow instead."

"I can stop breaking," I say, fully aware that I sound like an alcoholic. *I can stop drinking whenever I want. . . .*

He says, "Jonah."

People do this—say my name strong and forceful, like the two syllables and a serious look will give them some sort of power over me. It's just a name. It's not like it means anything.

He says, "Jonah. You can't go home until you work with me."

He's working off the assumption that going home is my goal.

"Where's Leah?" I say.

"Hmm?"

"We haven't seen her this morning. She wasn't at breakfast or lunch."

"I don't know anything that I can share right now."

I glare at him and scratch the knee of my jeans.

"So, what are we going to do here, Jonah? Are you ready to start constructing some new behavior?"

I say, "I don't know anything that I can share right now."

He writes something on his clipboard, and I hear applause in my head. Jonah: 1. Mental Health: 0.

thirty-six

NAOMI CALLS WHEN I'M IN THE LOUNGE AFTER lunch. We're all crowded around the armchairs, worrying about Leah, when IMOAN appears on my caller ID.

"Hey, babe," I say, smiling at Mackenzie as she takes her post behind the desk.

Naomi's voice is comforting in its coarseness. "Well, you sound cheery."

I admit that, despite all the shit with Jess and Leah and the psychologist, I feel sort of cheery.

"I heard she's in the infirm," Belle announces on her way upstairs.

Tyler groans. "She better not have had a heart attack."

Stephen throws his hands over his head. "Tyler, don't say that."

"Anorexic girls have heart attacks all the time. It happens."

I try not to listen. "How's school?" I ask Naomi.

"Fine. And Jess is great," she adds before I can ask. "I've been keeping an eye on him."

"He's eating?"

"Yep. He kicked ass in the hockey game, honestly. He's doing great."

"That's awesome." I cover the mouthpiece and catch Annie's eye as she comes in from the courtyard, shuffling her feet against the ground. "Any news?"

She shakes her head.

"Jesse misses you," Naomi says. "Every time I talk to him all he'll say is how much he misses you."

"He's healthy."

"Yeah. And sad."

Belle runs in from the hallway. "She's in the infirmary."

"What happened?"

Her face is all red. "She broke her arm."

I drop the phone. "What?"

thirty-seven

THE DOCTOR GATHERS US ALL TOGETHER IN THE common room because he thinks we're worried about Leah.

"Because of her weight, her bones break very easily. Think of an old woman's." He straightens his glasses. "It's unfortunate, but not shocking, and she's going to recover just fine."

God, I'm like the angel of bad health. I leave, and Jesse gets well. I come here, and Leah breaks her bones. I wonder if there's an angel of bad health in the Bible, and I wonder if he got swallowed by a big fish or shoved from place to place like a pinball.

We're sitting in a circle in the lounge. I stare at my lap, but I know everyone's watching me.

Tyler mumbles, "For the good of the group, right?"

I shake my head. "That's not what I meant."

I feel so shaky and sore I think I'm going to pass out. My broken hand is throbbing.

"Leah should be home from the hospital tonight. Hopefully she won't have to coincide with any of those Halloween burn victims." He smiles, and Stephen and I flinch because we don't like the words "burn" and "Halloween."

"You've all got exercise period in ten minutes," the doctor says. "Why don't you go get changed while I speak to Jonah?"

I clasp my hands between my legs while the others clear the room. Tyler squeezes my good shoulder on his way out.

The doctor scoots close to me. It's the first time he's managed to make me feel honestly comfortable. "You know why I want to talk to you, right?"

I nod. "I didn't tell Leah to do it."

"But you understand how this looks."

"Yeah."

"Could you have said anything? To encourage her to do this?"

"I . . . explained to Mackenzie. She overheard."

"Mackenzie?"

"One of the volunteers."

"Right. Right." He chews his lip. "The principle of this home is that you help each other heal, okay? If there's a chance you could be interfering with the recovery of another patient . . . you understand that we have to take that very seriously."

"Yeah."

"Just . . . be careful, all right, Jonah? We don't want to have to put you in isolation."

I look up.

He smiles. "Just watch yourself, all right? Everything'll be fine. Leah's gonna heal up nicely, and you'll be home in no time, all right?"

"Okay. Thank you."

Annie's waiting for me in my room.

"Hi," I say.

She hands me a little slip of paper. I read the note: *I believe in you.*

I spin from the shoulders up. "Thank you."

I think.

My nausea claims get me out of exercise period, but they still drag me out of bed for art and dinner. All I want to do is sleep. The psychiatrist lets me out of our session early so I can rest, and I crash until Mackenzie comes in to check my vitals.

"You're the talk of the nurse's station," she says.

"Seriously?"

"Yep. Everyone's gossiping about your little mission."

"It's not a mission," I slur, my head in my pillow. "Just a few broken bones."

"Are they hurting you?"

I hold up the hand. "Just this one."

"Want anything for it?"

I shake my head.

My blood pressure's low, and I'm staring to wonder if it has anything to do with my stomachache and headache and overwhelming dizziness.

"You're not feeling well," she says. "Do you want a nurse?"

"I just want to sleep."

And I do, and then I wake up to the welcome home party for Leah. I stumble out of my bed into the common room, barefoot, scrubbing my eyes with my pulsating hand.

"Jonah!" Leah throws her broken and unbroken arms around my neck. "Look!" she shows me the cast, the marks where Tyler and Stephen and Belle and Annie have already signed their names.

I sway and they pull me onto the carpet.

"I feel so much better," she says.

I say, "The point isn't to *feel* better."

"But I do." She flexes her good arm. "I feel . . . stronger. Don't you guys? I did it for you guys."

Everyone nods.

Leah's smile grows. Her mouth is too big and she's all lit from inside. She looks like a jack-o'-lantern.

"Not feeling well," I mumble.

"Oh, Jonah." Leah collects me from the floor and steers me down the hall to my room. The hallway stretches in front of me like a tendon. "You'll be okay," she says. "It's just been a while since you've broken anything, yeah? Feeling a little withdrawn?"

"Don't need to break anymore."

"Shh. It's okay."

I sleep like a tiger and then someone's hands are on my shoulders, and I just want them to leave me alone. I don't want to think about this. I'm so sick of thinking.

"Jonah. Jonah."

It's Tyler. I sit up. My eyes sting like I've soaked them in acid.

Tyler's a film noir character in the half-light from my window. "Look," he says, and holds out his hand.

His ring finger is bent and swollen.

I grab his hand and dig around in my backpack until I find a roll of medical tape. "You're going to be fine,"

I say. "Don't let the doctor see. Please. Please don't let him see."

He smiles like a maniac. "Jonah," he says. "The good of the group, right? You're a fucking genius."

Then it's Halloween.

thirty-eight

JESSE. I WALK OUT OF ARTS AND CRAFTS THE NEXT morning, not perfect, but not altogether worse for wear, and there he is, chatting with Mackenzie at the desk while he signs the visitor's clipboard.

I approach him. "You skipped school to be here?"

He shrugs. "At least there's no chance of Mom and Dad bothering us. And there's a notable lack of shrieking babies."

"Rather extreme, brother." I remember last time and say, "You want to go outside?"

I take him through the back doors, out to the courtyard. We sit on the rickety bench, and Jesse drags a stick across the ground.

"They really give you a lot of freedom, here, don't they?"

"Yeah."

"Couldn't you just run away?"

I point toward the gates that block us from the real world and shake my bracelet. "Sensors go off if I get too close. It's an illusionary freedom. How's everything?"

"Fine." He takes my arm and compares my crazy-bracelet to the med-alert tags on his wrist.

"Healthy?"

"Yes, Jonah." He shakes back his tags and spies the basketball by the side of the court. "Hey, you want to play?"

"Is this just revenge for asking if you're healthy? Okay. I didn't mean it. I don't care if you're healthy. Want a peanut butter sandwich?"

"Shut up." He stands up and throws the ball at me. "Let's go."

Jesse got taller than me when we were six and seven. That was also the last year I could beat him in any kind of sport. But I give it my all, just like always, because it's what he expects even though I'm not feeling very basketbally at the moment. And it's not as if I can move much.

He fakes left and almost sends me toppling. "Reflexes, brother. Haven't improved, haveya?"

"Oh, hush."

He holds the ball over his head. "No toes. Can't jump."

"I'll do it."

"Don't." He dribbles right and throws the ball toward the hoop like he's punishing it. It sinks right through the net.

He smiles and flicks a bit of sweat off his forehead.

"You terrify me."

He retrieves the ball and offers his other arm to me. "Want to go? I'll pick you up."

"You could not pick me up with one arm."

"Hell yeah, I could." He grabs me around the waist, under the sling, and lifts me a full foot off the ground. "Hurting your ribs?"

"Uh-uh. Holy shit, you're strong." I take the ball from him, balance it in my one hand, and shoot. "Score."

"Yep. Putting you down. Watch your toes, okay?"

He could keep playing for ages, I know, but he senses I'm getting tired and guides me over to the bench. "How's everything here?" he asks.

I consider telling him about Tyler and Leah, then decide that would be a really, really bad idea. "Fine," I say. "The people here are wearing on me. I kind of want to come home."

"Kind of?" He stretches his legs out. "I miss you like fuckass."

"I know. But you're doing okay without me."

"Stop saying that." Jess's cell phone timer goes off and he pops a few pills into his mouth. "You look exhausted."

"I haven't been sleeping much."

"Yeah, me neither." He shifts and pulls his legs onto the bench. "So when are you coming home?"

"It's sort of hard to say. The psychiatrist doesn't think I'm ready." I pull on my fingers. "Doesn't believe me when I say I'm not breaking anymore."

"But you aren't, are you?"

I shake my head.

"But he doesn't believe you?"

"He said nothing's changed. Said there's no real reason for me to change my behavior, and that people don't just change without motivation."

"He's keeping you here to spout philosophies at you?"

"I just don't understand what he expects me to change. That's the whole damn problem, is that I can't change anything."

Jess scratches his cheek. "Maybe I could talk to him. Tell him we need you at home?"

"Stop scratching. And you're not going to convince anybody. You got to just wait it out, Jess. They're treating me well. Give me, like, a week to convince them I'm not crazy, and I'll be at home making you sick just like always."

He scratches his wrist. "What'd you say?"

"Nothing. Why are you scratching so much?"

He shrugs.

"You okay?"

He shrugs again, and I know what that means. And he starts clearing his throat. Shit.

"All right," I say. "Come inside and wash your hands. You probably just touched something."

He nods. He's making those I-trust-you eyes.

"You have the Epi? Just in case?"

"Uh-huh."

"All right. Come on. You're okay." I haul him up and lead him through the doors. "Mackenzie," I say. "Do you have a bathroom on this floor we can use?"

She makes speed-of-light eye contact with me. I bite my lip.

She says, "Just bring him upstairs. It's fine. I'll clear it."

"Thanks, you."

She nods.

Once we're in the elevator, I give Jesse a real examination. His eyes are red and swollen, but he's not too broken out. "I think you're allergic to this building."

He squeezes his runny nose. "What a surprise."

I bring him to the bathroom I share with Tyler and help him splash his face with water.

"You're wheezing a little bit," I say. "Is this going to be a big thing?"

God please no please no please no not *again*.

He inhales, slowly. "Just let me sit in your room for a while, okay?"

I bring him into my room and we sit on the floor, our backs against the bed. He puts his head on my shoulder and closes his eyes.

Tyler peeks in, his taped-up fingers on the door frame. "Hey," he says.

I give him an apologetic smile and mouth, *Go away*.

He points at Jesse. "He okay?"

"He's great. Can we get a minute, Tyler?"

He nods and whispers, "Sorry" on his way out.

"Who was that?" Jesse asks.

"Tyler. Just one of the boys here."

"What happened to his hand?"

"Don't worry about it." I feel Jess's heartbeat on my shoulder, and it's slow and steady. Which could be good or bad, depending on how serious this reaction is. "You're fine." I grip his hand. "Everything's fine."

I feel my heart going double time to his.

Please be okay.

Please be okay.

He sneezes into my shirt. "Please be okay," I say.

"Okay."

"God, Jess, I'm sorry. Wait." I find an extra dose of Benadryl in my backpack and make him take it. He keeps snuffling for a few minutes, but his breathing comes back and the whites of his eyes lighten and I see the reaction slow and then stop.

"Y'okay?" I say.

"Yeah."

Fuck, why did I make him come here? He was perfectly healthy, and I drag him here when I *know* this place is bad for him. I could kill myself.

"You sure you're going to be fine?"

"Positive. But I should probably go."

"Of course."

I get Jesse off the floor and dust him off. I put my hand on his chest and make him breathe, check his jaw for hives, make him open his mouth so I can look at his throat . . . just all the shit you have to do.

He's fine.

"You should probably just call next time," I tell him, and my stomach hurts.

And he looks like his does too. "I need to see you."

"I know you do, Jess, but—"

"Jonah!" Mackenzie's voice rings through the hallway like an alarm bell. I hear every muscle clenched in her throat. "Jonah, come here!"

She's in the hall on her knees, clutching her arm. Her wrist is swollen and turning purple.

I say, "Did you . . . fall?"

Jesse skids beside me. "Oh my God."

She keeps sputtering.

I drop to my knees next to Mackenzie. "What did you do?" I grab the tops of her arms and shake her. "What the fuck did you do?"

"I slipped," she says. "It was an accident! It was just—"

Jesse's white against the wall. "Oh my God."

I shout, "Jesse, sit down!"

"What the hell is going on here?"

The unfamiliar voice breaks up all our screaming. No one speaks while I turn around.

A nurse stands above us. Her huge eyes dart from Mackenzie's broken wrist to illegal visitor Jesse. To me.

I'm crazy dizzy and I barely remember to tell the nurse not to touch Jesse as she forces him downstairs.

I'm crazy dizzy and I don't know what happens to

Mackenzie. I just know the psychiatrist stands over me and smiles this wicked smile and says, "Well, well, Jonah."

I just know they take me in the elevator and hit the 3.

thirty-nine

IT TURNS OUT ISOLATION IS WORSE THAN ELECTRO-shock therapy.

I feel like Rapunzel. Except no long hair.

And there is one door and one window. But the door is locked and the window is high and instead of curtains it has bars.

And through the window all you can see are skeletons of cherry trees. This is what they were hiding behind those trees. Third floor.

I hope Jesse's okay.

This room is much bigger than my last. There's no carpet, just an empty bookshelf and a cot. A tiny little intercom. Just tile floor and bare walls.

I sit on the floor with my shirt off, hoping the chill off the plaster can cool me down. And every time I worry about Jesse I start shaking even harder.

I've got to get out of here.

Jesse had hives when he left. He could have been driving home and his throat could have closed up and he could have crashed and it could have been all. My. Fault.

This room would be so much less scary if it were smaller.

I pound my cast against the floor. My swollen hand fights back. "Tyler!" I shout. "Tyler, I'm in fucking isolation! Get me out of here!"

The intercom buzzes and the psychiatrist says, "Jonah, quiet. It's only a few days."

I'm trembling so hard I hear my backbone hitting the wall.

"We can't take the risk of you hurting more people," he says.

I think if I'm going to keep on living, everyone's just going to have to accept that I am going to hurt people.

I start crying, and the tears are even hotter than my face. "It's not on purpose!" I shout. "Tyler!"

"He can't hear you," the intercom says. "You might as well just quiet down and try to get some rest." The microphone clicks off.

My parents would come down with a fucking lawsuit if they knew what these people were doing to me. I wonder what everyone downstairs would say. I wonder if they know.

I wonder what Jesse would say. I wonder what Charlotte would say.

I wonder if she'd realize, finally, that some people are crazier than me.

I can't believe they took my cell phone.

Charlotte. God, I need her so badly it's hurting in the back of my head and there's got to be a way I've got to have another chance with her there's got to be a way I can get out of here and—

A voice says, "Jonah?"

I snap my eyes open, but it's just the intercom.

"This is Nurse Bluser, Jonah. I've been assigned to your case."

I say, "Hi."

"You ready to admit what you've done, Jonah?"

"What?"

"What did you do to Leah and Mackenzie?"

"I didn't do *anything*."

My teeth are chattering, so I put my shirt on and crawl into the bed. The mattress is ridged and smells like urine.

She keeps talking, and I cover my ears up tight. I toss back and forward like I really think I can sleep. I sing, badly, to a Weezer song.

I have no clue how much time passes between the brutal singing and when I hear a key in the lock of my prison.

But I sit straight up, and the sweaty sheets fall right off my shoulders.

It's Mackenzie. She's out of her volunteer polo and is wearing a T-shirt and jeans. Her wrist's in a splint. She probably went to one of those corporate hospitals that can't figure out how to set and cast on the same day.

She holds her fingers to her lips and then edges the door shut. She takes a screwdriver out of her pocket and carefully disconnects the intercom. It lifts off the wall and hangs from a bunch of wires, and she snips them all with a pair of nail scissors.

"We don't have much time," she says.

"Hi," I say, and then I can't stop saying it. "Hi. Hi. Hi. Hi."

She comes to my bed and puts her hand all over my forehead and the back of my neck.

"Is your brother okay?" she says.

"I've got to find out, yeah?" My heart is screaming inside my chest.

"Uh-huh. God, you're sweaty."

"Mackenzie, Mackenzie. You're letting me out, right?"

She leans very close to me. "There are stairs down the hall. Code for the lock. It's Four-four-two-five. Run down the stairs, three flights, and you'll get to a back door. Don't stop running. Get the hell out of here."

"Okay," I whisper.

I head toward the door, and she says, "Wait." I turn around and she hugs me.

She cuts my bracelet off and says, "Thank you."

"For what?"

She just smiles, and my stomach churns.

"No," I say. "It was an accident. This isn't my fault." I bend over and cough, and she puts her hand on my back. "None of this is my fault," I insist. "I've got to get out of here."

She opens the door, and I run down the hall. My breath rags and threatens to make me cough again. I no longer give a shit about my broken toes. Any second I'm sure I'm going to hear sirens. . . . Any second they're going to drag me back. . . . They're going to tie me up. . . .

4425.

The door won't open.

Oh, God. I've been set up.

She's working for them. Her wrist isn't really broken. It's all an act and I'm screwed I'm screwed I'm fucking screwed.

4425442544254425

The latch gives.

Never mind.

I almost hit myself with the door, I'm pulling so hard.

Mackenzie is somewhere and I hear her voice. "Run, Jonah!" and I don't know why she had to say my name. I don't know why everyone has to say my name.

I stop halfway down the stairs so I can breathe. The stairs are dark and wet and awful, and I keep expecting light at the end.

But it's night.

I am Jonah. I spent three days in dark hell and now I'm out. Sputtering and alive.

I break through the bottom door, out of the home, into Halloween.

forty

I WADE THROUGH MUSHY WEEDS FOR TEN MINUTES before I reach the bus stop. I pant and lean against the cubicle and wait for the bus with a witch and some kind of animal-slut.

When I climb aboard, the bus driver nods. "Cool costume."

Since when is a cast a costume? I guess the whole sweaty/lurchy thing helps, though.

I sit down and try not to look at the freaky people who ride the bus on Halloween. Before, bus passengers always looked narcoleptic. Now they're so antsy I'd believe they're all on speed, and I have a hard time convincing myself that they're not psych-ward spies, hiding cameras and tape recorders behind the masks and provocative costumes.

I swallow and brush dirt off my jeans. Concentrate.

Charlotte lives right by the school.

Right by the bus stop.

It's not hard.

Really, it's my best option. It's not as if I can go home. Please. When the police are looking for you, the last place you can go is home. I assume it's the same for psychopathic psychologists.

You can never go home.

You're a mental health outlaw.

My broken hand grinds with every speed bump.

This might not be the worst thing. I'll miss Jess, and Will, but they'll do better without me. Charlotte and I could run away together. After I convince her I'm not crazy.

We could have kids and name them Jesse and Naomi.

I get off the bus and walk across the parking lot to school. A few freshmen in stupid *Scream* masks are egging the science lab. They startle when they see me.

"Don't throw eggs, you idiots," I say.

They bristle. "Who the fuck do you think you are?"

"I'm the fucking police. Some people are allergic to eggs, assholes. Clean this up."

One kid actually does. What a fucking loser.

The deeper I get into the residential areas, the crazier the crowds get. I pass Frankensteins and ballerinas and zombies. I pass people much, much too old to be dressed up. More teenagers who use Halloween as an excuse to get naked.

The cold air is like my mother's hand on my cheek when I'm sick. I stumble on my toes and scrape my palm when I catch myself. My broken hand explodes like fireworks.

Get up.

No one heads toward Charlotte's neighborhood except these two teenagers, a pirate and a fairy. I watch them from a few feet behind. She has a clay pumpkin full of candy dangling from one tiny pink hand, and holds his white glove with the other.

They don't know I'm following them, and that makes me happy and sad all in the pit of my stomach.

Then they stop and kiss under a streetlight, and my knees almost fall off.

The tiny little fairy, with the purple dress and eyeliner and delicate tights—it's baseball-cap-hardass Naomi.

And the pirate.

The pirate with Naomi's tongue in his mouth.

It's Jesse.

forty-one

MY STOMACH'S ABOUT TO COME OUT MY NOSE.

"What are you *doing*?"

They rip around to me and their mouths fall open. Jesse's hat covers half his shocked expression. He says, "Jonah?"

I grab his arm and pull him toward me. "Spit!"

"Jonah—"

"Spit!"

He spits into the grass, and Naomi says, "Hey!"

He looks at her. "Nomy—"

"Shush!" I scream, and I won't take my hands off Jesse. "Did she wash her mouth out first?"

"What are you doing out of the—"

I grab the pumpkin out of Naomi's hand. "You've got candy in here! You've got chocolate and peanuts and—"

She snatches all the Jesse-poison back. "I didn't eat any of it! Come on, I wouldn't do that!"

Jesse says, "What the hell are you doing here?"

"You can't just go around kissing girls!"

He exhales. "I can look after my—"

"Do you just want to die? Is that it?" I think I'm going to strangle him.

"*Shut up!*" He covers his ears. "Shut up shut up shut up!"

He breathes hard. Naomi and I stare at him silently. I check his wrists and neck and cheeks, looking for hives.

Naomi puts her hand on his back.

I snap. "No, don't comfort him!"

"Jonah, shut up!" she says.

I wave my cast in Jesse's face like I'm going to hit him. "This is not about your fucking independence. You can't . . ." I'm so dizzy. "You can't just—especially not dirty girls like—"

Naomi takes her hand off Jesse and looks at me. "What did you just call me?"

"I—"

WHAM.

It takes me a second to realize what she hit me with.

The damn clay pumpkin. Candy flies to the ground and Jess jumps out the way.

The pressure in my face is unbelievable.

"Fuck," I whisper, pressing my hand against my cheek.

Jesse whirls to Naomi. "What the hell did you just do?"

"You heard what he said!"

Jesse looks at me. "Are you okay?"

I breathe in and out, slowly, holding my face as tightly as I can. "Did you hear something crack?"

Jesse pulls me into the light and touches the space under my eye. I whine.

"You broke his cheekbone," he whispers.

Naomi's chin shakes. "I didn't—"

"You broke my fucking brother's cheekbone! What the fuck were you thinking?"

"He called me—"

"Yeah, so yell at him! Hate him! Don't fucking break him!"

I hold him back because I'm afraid he's got to hit her. He shakes me off. He might not be on her side, but he's sure as hell not on mine, either.

I almost fall over, and he says, "Look, you're sick. I'm taking you home."

"I have to talk to Charlotte."

"No. You need to go home and tell me what the fuck you're doing out of the psych ward." He points the way we came. "My car's in the next neighborhood. Come on."

We leave Naomi crying under the streetlight.

forty-two

JESS OPENS THE FRONT DOOR, AND I'M HIT WITH baby screams. He pays the frazzled babysitter and sends her home. Then he brings me into the baby's room and sets me on the floor. "Wait here."

I huddle in the corner and put my fingers on my cheek. I close my eyes to Will's sobs.

"Can you open your mouth enough for this?" he says, holding up the thermometer.

I can, just barely, but it *hurts*. Jesse crams it into my mouth.

"You had no right," he says, ripping off pieces of his costume until he's just my brother again. "Absolutely no right to come and fucking interrupt us, Jonah. That is not your place."

I was protecting him.

Ungrateful little bastard.

"I'm sixteen years old. I know how my body works, okay? I know what I have to do. I don't *need* this anymore."

And there it is. I fucking knew it. He doesn't need me.

"I was worried about you," I slur.

He looks straight at me and bites his lips. "I know, brother. Man . . . I know." He pushes my bangs out of my eyes and takes the thermometer out of my mouth as it starts to beep. "103.4. Shit."

"Yeah. I don't feel that great."

He goes to the closet and finds an extra quilt. "Come here." He brings me to the rocking chair and covers me all the way over my head. The squeak of the chair as I shiver reminds me of him on the rowing machine.

I think that I'm home free.

Then he says, "Too bad for you Mom and Dad aren't home. They'd probably be too concerned to drill you for information."

Now I don't feel hidden well enough at all.

"How the hell did you get out of the psych hospital, Jonah?"

"They put me in isolation. It was awful. The volunteer helped me escape."

"After you convinced her to break her wrist?"

"I didn't do it." My voice shakes with my body. "I didn't do it."

"Jonah, what is going on?"

I say, "I did it for you."

His voice finds me through the quilt with intense clarity. "No! This isn't about me! Stop pretending your whole life is about me!"

I think I'm crying but I can't tell.

It's so humid and sticky under these sheets. I throw them all off.

"I've got to go," he says.

"Where are you going?"

He's pacing back and forth, his hands in his hair. "I've got to try to make things okay with Naomi, man!"

Will picks up his screaming.

"She hit me!"

"Jonah."

"I'm sick!"

"Shhh." He stops pacing and heads for the crib.

"Don't hold him," I say.

"SHUT UP! Stop telling me not to hold him! It's not

like you're going to help him if I don't! You talk all this *shit* about family and then you . . ."

"What are you—"

He covers his ears with his palms. "God, man, I can't do this right now, all right? Having you around when I'm sick is not worth you making me think I'm sick when I'm not, okay? I want to be a fucking *human*, and I can't keep arguing the same fucking things with you, Jonah! You have a fuckload more family members you could worry about, and this is not my life!" He tightens his hands. "This can't be my life."

"I'm trying to keep you alive, you asshole!"

Jesse, stop covering your ears. Jesse, listen to me.

I start to recoil under the quilt but Jess yanks me back into the room, back into life. One of his muscular hands grabs the front of my neck and pushes back on my throat. I am choking on my own vocal cords.

It is a relief not to breathe.

"This needs to stop," he says. He bites down on his tongue.

My eyes water.

"I am not going—" he stops and swallows. "I am not going to die. I have shit to take care of and you stop making me think I'm going to die."

Will's room spins and the baby is upside down. I latch

around Jesse's wrist and try to pull him off me, but he won't budge. I try to cough and the pressure makes my broken face explode.

Jesse's going to kill me.

"Stop telling me I'm going to die," he says.

I blink and he releases me, returns to his pacing. I rub my chest and cough without fanfare. My face aches.

When I've stored some breath, I say, "Stay here. We can talk about this."

"No! Jesus, I can't talk about this anymore, okay? I've got, like, life. And you need to back off. Okay." He stops and faces me. "Okay. You're sick. So you stay here. And you listen to the fucking baby cry, okay?"

"Jess—"

"Maybe you'll try to help him! Who the fuck knows?"

"I am trying!" I close my eyes against the fuzziness and snap my hands over my head. "I'm trying I'm trying I'm trying I'm trying."

But Jesse's gone.

He left me here.

I curl up and hum, but none of it helps. I hug my quilt and my chair and I try to be happy that I'm home, but I know any second I'm going to hear a sort of dog-whistle siren that only crazy people can hear, and the men in white coats will come and take me away.

And Jesse's gone, and now I have nowhere to go but Charlotte's.

And I can't walk that far.

In fact, about two minutes later I throw up on the floor.

I've thrown up a few times before, but it never hurt like this. With the wires in my jaw, I'm very nearly choking.

"Ohhh my God," I groan.

I consider calling Jesse. He's thrown up enough times that it doesn't bother him anymore.

Or I could call Mom and Dad.

But I don't want them.

I just want the girl with the white teeth and the flowers in her hair. Is that so much to ask? Is it so incredibly more than I deserve?

Yes.

Will's screams tumble into my ears. The smell of my vomit burns the inside of my nostrils like my brain is being cauterized.

A smell-lobotomy.

Jonah, think.

Fever + broken bones = infection.

What's that word?

Oh. Right. Osteomyelitis.

Symptoms: pain and swelling at the infection site.

I look at my fucking broken hand.

Fever. Nausea.

Treatment:

IV antibiotics.

Amputation.

Death.

So this is it. This is a moment. This is an I-have-nothing-to-lose moment.

I stand up and my knees click with my shaking.

"Wait," I say. "Wait." I go to the crib and look down at Will, look at his purple baby face.

"You can come with me, if you want," I say.

He cries. I'll take that to mean *yes*.

"We're a family, right?" I talk to him all the way out of the house. "Come on, Will. It's cold. You need a coat, okay?" I pull his purple coat over his arms. "I have a fever, so I'm all right, but you need a coat. Stay warm, okay, Will?"

I take the cordless phone. "I need to call Charlotte," I tell him as I shut the front door behind us. "Oh, look. It's raining."

I dial her number as Will and I walk down the street. The raindrops are so heavy and thick like hail, or God-spit.

A girl's voice says, "Hello?"

"Charlotte?"

"No. This is Ellie. Her sister."

Oh. Mini-Charlotte. I guess she does have a name after all.

Ellie's voice reminds me of Charlotte's, and it's like a milkshake on my sore throat.

"Is Charlotte there?"

"Uh-uh. She's at a party. Who is this?"

"Jonah."

"Oh. Hi, Jonah."

"Hi."

She's quiet and I hear her breathe. She's got these loud inhales like Jesse, and I wonder if she has asthma.

"How are you doing?" she says.

I shift Will against my chest. He's getting wet. I should have brought his hat. I shouldn't have taken him out. He's supposed to stay in the house, my parents say. What if he gets sick?

I say, "I'm good."

She says, "You know, my dad was in an institution for a little while. Before I was born."

The rain picks up, and I feel like it should be snowing.

"He's okay now," she says.

"That's good. Good. We should all be okay now."

I open my mouth to catch the invisible snowflakes. My cheekbone stretches like angry Silly Putty. Rain covers my eyes. I wonder if the phone will explode in the rain, if it'll catch me on fire.

Why not die?

I've done enough, and it doesn't sound like a compliment.

Will whinnies and rubs his head on my chest. He's got to stop crying. For Mom and Dad and Jesse and me and himself, he needs to stop crying and it's up to me.

"How's your brother?" she says.

"Which one?"

"Jesse."

My chest pounds. "Oh, Ellie, listen. I'm so sorry. I'm so sorry I'm so sorry."

"What?"

"I should have told him you liked him. I should have let it happen. I did a lot of things with him, okay? And he doesn't . . . I shouldn't have."

"Okay."

She answers me like she is a fantastic actress in a play. Like she knows exactly when it's her turn to speak, and when she needs to stop and let me ramble.

But it's hard to hear her over Will.

"I messed up a lot with him." I tighten my grip. "I'm trying to be better. . . . I'm trying something else now. . . ."

"Jonah, are you okay?"

I say, "Can you tell Charlotte something for me?"

"All right."

"I don't really know what's going to happen next," I say.

I don't know if I'm going to get septic. I don't know if they're going to amputate my hand. I don't know if I'm crazy. Or if I'm going to die. Or if Jesse's going to die. Or when.

I keep walking and walking. "But can you tell her I love her?"

"What?"

I think I'm going to throw up again. "And that I really want to be with her? And that we can make it nice and not stupid. And I should have told her a long time ago, and I'm sorry I waited—"

The phone is so cold against my ear. Ellie starts to speak and the connection dies.

"Hello?"

Too far away from the house, I guess. Shouldn't have left my cell phone at the psych ward.

I'm too far away from the ground. I'm going to fall and I'm too far away. I put my forehead on the ground, holding Will like he's a yelling teddy bear.

No. No. Shit.

I think I'm going to throw up.

I think I'm going to—

It can't end like this.

Not like this. Not on the street. Not without making sure Will's okay.

All I can hear is the footstep sound of rain on the street. The rest is silent, because Will has stopped crying.

He stopped crying. I feel his body, so cold against my fever-cheek. He licks a raindrop off my chin.

The pavement digs into my forehead.

I made him stop crying. Maybe it can be o—

Will coos, "Jo."

I pretend he's saying my name. I pretend he's calling me back.

forty-three

THE FIRST FEELING IS DUST.

His voice slides to me. "I know you're awake. And don't think I'm not mad at you just because of this life-threatening infection thing."

I raise the corners of my mouth. "Hi, Jesse."

"Hi. Open your eyes."

I do, so quietly I'm barely aware of any movement. The white sheets under me crunch like they're made of butcher paper.

Everything is slow and white.

Jesse sits by my bed, his shirtsleeves rolled to his elbows, muscular hands folded in his lap.

I say, "I figured the first time I woke up there'd be people standing over my bed holding flowers."

"You've woken up a few times before. You were just too feverish to remember."

"Oh." I blink and feel my eyelashes. "How long have I been here?"

"Just a few hours."

"And how the hell did I get here?"

"You called Ellie. Ellie called Charlotte. Charlotte called me."

"Oh."

"And I found you and Will sleeping in a puddle half a block away from the house. Brought you here—"

"Is Will all right?"

"He's fine." Jess laughs. "Better than—hey, you all right?"

The second feeling is pain.

"You okay?" he says.

I bite my lips.

My hand hurts. The IV in my other hand hurts. My head hurts. But it's all so far away, so I nod. One of my cords beeps and stops beeping every time I make a fist. I do this for a few seconds, watching my fingers clench. I'm alive. Dead people can't make fists. Dead people have nothing to fight.

I chew the tip of my tongue, feeling my throat choke up.

I still have both my hands. And I'm still alive.

The third feeling is exhilaration.

I'm still alive.

The walls are clean and pale. The television at the foot of my bed shows some idiot getting tattooed. I hear quiet, way-away voices.

"You scared the hell out of us," Jess says.

"I know."

"You've got to stop doing that."

"Okay."

"Got to stop fighting us now."

I don't say anything.

He rubs his jaw. "Look outside."

I turn my head toward the big window that divides me and the hallway world. And there's Charlotte.

The holly in her hair presses against the window. Her brown eyes stick to mine. I'm still alive. And even if I wasn't, her face would be enough.

Jesse and everyone melt away.

The fourth feeling is falling in love.

This can be my fight. I can fight for her.

And through the window there's Dad, praying by himself, his lips moving to something he trusts. There's Mom, walking Will up and down the hall while he sleeps on her shoulder, his face pink like a real baby's. Silent.

And I know, I know everything is far from perfect, but it's hard to care.

"We've got to tell a doctor you're lucid," Jesse says.

I swallow back everything. "Where's Naomi?"

Throat-clearing. I turn my head to the other side and there she is.

She's back in her grody clothes, baseball cap perched on her head. She's wearing earrings. I wonder where she got them.

Her eyes flick from Jesse to me. "Hey, partner."

"Hey."

"How you feeling?"

I can't remember, but I say, "Better," because it sounds like the right answer.

She says, "Not to steal your thunder, but Jess and I decided we're not gonna let you fuck us up."

I close my eyes against a new pain wave. "He's allergic to latex."

Jesse smacks me.

"I'm just saying. Before you get your freak on." *Ugh*.

Naomi says, "You want to see Charlotte?"

She smiles hopefully through the window.

I want to, but I'm so, so tired. My face falls down with my eyes.

"Let him sleep," Jess says, "There'll be time."

I say, "Tell her—"

"You can tell her later, brother."

Jess takes Naomi by the hand and pulls her outside. I can't ask if she washed her hands—I can't ask it anymore. My mouth is too heavy with too much medication and feelings and shit.

They take their seats on the bench outside and mumble to Charlotte, mumble to Mom and Dad. I keep my eyes open. I will watch them until I fall asleep.

I will watch them because I need to.

"Let him sleep," Jesse is telling Mom. "He's going to be fine."

I'm going to be fine, Jesse says.

He says, "I'll take Will home, if you want. My car's here."

Dad sits down next to him. "Why didn't you call an ambulance?"

My brother crosses his arms, his jaw set. "Because I got him here faster."

Charlotte taps on the glass so I'll look at her. Her lips move and I'm too blurry, I can't read the words—but I read every bit of the smile and the eye-sparkle.

We're going to be fine, Charlotte says.

Dad says, "You did good, Jesse."

Did he . . . Jesse, shit, did he lift me off the street? Did he put me in his car? Did he rescue Will and me from certain death? After I fucked up his life?

But Jess smiles and ducks his head, his cheeks glowing like they've been pinched. "I did what I had to do."

Mom says, "You saved his life."

Mom is so literal.

And Jesse knows it, and he humors her and says, "Yeah." He bites his lips together and looks in at my room. He says. "Yeah, now we're even."

He stands up and takes the baby, bounces him on his hockey-player's hip.

The fifth feeling is healing.

Or if it's not, it's close enough.

No regrets.

Check Your PULSE

Simon & Schuster's **Check Your Pulse**
e-newsletter delivers current updates on
the hottest titles, exciting sweepstakes, and
exclusive content from your favorite authors.

Visit **TEEN.SimonandSchuster.com** to
sign up, post your thoughts, and find out what
every avid reader is talking about!

Margaret K. McElderry Books

Simon & Schuster
Books for Young Readers

SIMON
PULSE

About the Author

If all goes well, Hannah Moskowitz will be out of high school by the time you read this. She can't cook, likes to play dress up, and has never broken a bone. *Break* is her first novel. Learn more at UntilHannah.com.